SHADOWS OVER BALINOR

Read all the Unicorns of Balinor books:

UNICORNS OF BALINOR

SHADOWS OVER BALINOR

MARY STANTON

AN
APPLE
PAPERBACK

SCHOLASTIC INC
New York Toronto London Auckland Sydney
Mexico City New Delhi Hong Kong

Cover illustration by D. Craig

ISBN 0-439-16787-6

12 11 10 9 8 7 6 5 4 3 2   0 1 2 3 4 5/0

Printed in the U.S.A.   40
First Scholastic printing, May 2000

For Harry and Jen

SHADOWS OVER BALINOR

1

Acomet trailed pale fire across the evening sky over the Celestial Valley. Beneath the light of the stars, the Celestial unicorns danced for joy.

The unicorns leaped, horns glittering in the light shed by the stars and comet. They moved in a triumphant circle, silken manes flowing to their knees, tails flagged high and proud. Atalanta, the Dreamspeaker, stood at the center, neck arched, dark purple eyes glowing with love and happiness. "Dance on!" she cried in her low, sweet voice. And the Celestial unicorns responded with higher leaps and gleeful pirouettes.

Tonight there was no need to fear their ancient enemy the Shifter. Princess Arianna and her Bonded unicorn, the Sunchaser, had defeated the Shifter and his army. The Celestial Valley was safe. And Balinor was free!

"Hail, Arianna!" Rednal shouted. The giant

crimson stallion reared in a levade, his forelegs raking the air.

"Hail!" the Rainbow herd responded.

When the Rainbow herd assembled in sunlight, they formed a blaze of color. The jewels holding their horns glittered so brightly they rivaled the sun. But now the starlight muted the flame-shaded red band, the deep blues of the indigo band, and all the colors in between. The unicorns danced in silvery fire.

"And halt!" the Dreamspeaker said. With a murmur of their silken manes, a thrumming of hooves on the grass, the unicorns settled down and turned to her. Atalanta's crystal horn shone with the deep light of the stars themselves. "We are at peace!" she cried. "Let all sleep well tonight!"

Talking happily among themselves, the unicorns wandered off to curl up in the thick, sweet grass or to stand and doze until the sun rose over the Eastern Ridge. Atalanta watched them go, her heart filled with love for them and for the people and animals she guarded in the lands below the Celestial Valley. She would not sleep this night. The battle had been only recently won, and she needed time to consider what a peaceful future would bring.

She walked to the banks of the Imperial River and inhaled the fresh scent of the water. She cropped a few starflowers, delighting in their slightly astringent taste. Finally, she came to the path that led to the Watching Pool, the magical spot where she could observe the daily life of Balinor and her beloved subjects Arianna and her unicorn, the Sunchaser.

Should she watch tonight? Although their greatest enemy had been defeated, there was still a great deal to be done. The King and Queen of Balinor — kidnapped by the Shifter — were still missing. So were the two Royal Princes. Although Arianna had possession of the throne and the country was at peace, the months ahead would be filled with challenges and adventure.

But they were so much safer now that the greatest evil Balinor had ever known was out of the way!

Atalanta smiled to herself. Now that the balance of magic was restored to Balinor — and the Princess was in full command of her own personal powers — Atalanta could no longer walk the path from the moon to visit Arianna in person. But she could send her a dream tonight. A dream filled with love and reassurance that, while Arianna would not see Atalanta again, the Dreamspeaker would always be with her.

Atalanta walked to the pool with a light heart. She heard the whisper of the waterfall before she came to the waters themselves. Even the trickling falls sounded happy! She rounded the amethyst boulders that flanked the entrance and trotted to the stone ledge where she had stood so many times before.

The Watching Pool was still. Faint reflections of the stars marked the surface, and the faraway smudge of the comet was like a ghostly finger on the water. Atalanta bent her head until her horn just touched the water. An image appeared.

It was the Princess herself, asleep in her room at the Palace. All the worry and care of the past few months was gone from the young girl's face. She slept deeply, one hand tucked around the powerful magic Scepter. After the Shifter's defeat, Arianna had been up late, healing the wounded people and animals with the salves and medicines given to her by Dr. Bohnes.

A curled, furry shape at the foot of Arianna's bed meant that her loyal collie, Lincoln, was there. And very near, just outside her window, the great bronze unicorn, the Sunchaser, dozed quietly.

Then a shadow fell across Arianna's face. She stirred and murmured in her sleep. Atalanta stepped back. She looked up at the sky. The comet was larger. It hung there like a misshapen moon. And as she stared at it now, Atalanta could see that it was not at all what it had seemed at first. Behind the white light was a boiling mixture of color: bruised purple, black, dark brown, and polluted green. The comet grew larger. The shadow of the comet fell over the Watching Pool, masking the image of the sleeping Arianna.

What was this? Atalanta stiffened in alarm. "I call on Balinor," Atalanta said. The image in the pool widened until the Dreamspeaker could see the thatched cottages, the great sprawl of the Palace, and the fields and roads of the land. And the shadow fell over all of it. The shadow fell over Balinor itself.

No, Atalanta thought. *No. Not so soon. It isn't fair!*

Kraken.

Kraken was coming.

The Dreamspeaker trembled. A new evil was headed toward Balinor. And Arianna didn't know, couldn't know, about the danger of using the Royal Scepter in times like these. All magic calls to all magic. Each time she used the Scepter, Kraken would grow stronger. Those who worked for him would draw closer to Arianna herself.

And there was no easy way to warn her.

2

A small black cat pattered busily down the wide marble aisle of the Royal Mews in Balinor. Little more than a kitten, she carried her tail straight up as she went past the Royal unicorns in their stalls. She was thin, and her fur was patchy. A curious piece of rolled rope twisted around her neck, no more than a rag. But despite her rough appearance and ragged collar, she carried herself with all the authority of the Sunchaser himself, the Lord of the Animals in Balinor.

The sun was just up, and the air was soft. Sunlight touched the carved wooden stall doors with golden peach. There was a pleasant rhythmic sound of munching as the Royal unicorns ate their morning oats, and a comfortable scent of bedding and clean hay. But the little cat ignored it all. Suddenly, she crouched, nose twitching, fuzzy tail lashing back and forth. Her wide golden eyes narrowed as she sniffed the floor.

She jumped, batted at the air with her paws, then made a tiny sound like a whirring hummingbird. It was a ridiculously small sound in that vast and gorgeous place. She scratched one ear and trotted on.

Hmm, she thought with satisfaction, *anyone watching me will know what a good fighter I am after seeing those fast moves. But I'll have to work on that growl. It's not quite ferocious enough.*

A beautiful black unicorn with a sapphire blue jewel at the base of her horn watched as she proceeded down the aisle, so the little cat stuck her frizzy chest out and held her tail high. The bronze nameplate on the unicorn's door read TIERZA. As the cat went by, Tierza leaned over her half-door and asked, "What in the world are you up to, little one?"

The cat yowled in surprise and flew straight up in the air. She hadn't expected to be spoken to, not by a unicorn as important as this one must be! She landed on all four legs with a thump, shook herself, and said crossly, "Well, here's a fine thing! Scarin' me half to death."

She sat down abruptly, stuck out one hind leg, and began to groom around an ugly red scratch on her paw. Her ears twitched and she muttered, "Here's a cat mindin' her very own business. Just goin' about, finding some breakfast. And does she get to mind her very own business without getting the life scared out of her? No, she does not!" She made the hummingbird sound again and grumbled, "Unicorns!"

Tierza's dark brown eyes crinkled in amusement. The cat wished (not for the first time!) that her growl was more ferocious. And from the look on her face, the lovely unicorn could see how the cat's ribs stuck out beneath her carefully groomed fur. And although the scratches on her paws and sides had been cleaned up, they hadn't healed very well. The unicorn probably thought she was some stray looking for something to eat. The cat wriggled uncomfortably. She didn't need anyone's pity!

Tierza said gently, "Can I help you?"

"I don't need any help, thank you very much! Now that you've scared me to death by all that bellowing!"

The Royal unicorn in the stall across the aisle from Tierza pulled his head up from his bucket of oats and stared sternly at the cat. He was the color of rosewood and his silver horn had a dark rose jewel at its base.

"What's all the fuss?" he asked, looking at Tierza.

"Beecher," the cat read aloud, for that was the name on his stall door. The cat rolled over on her back and gazed at Beecher upside down. She narrowed her eyes in a fierce way and growled in her hummingbird voice, "You talkin' to me? You'd better be careful! Odie's my name and fightin's my game!"

Tierza snorted to keep from giggling. Beecher chuckled, shook his head, and went back to his grain. Odie rolled to her feet and started to swagger down the aisle again.

"If you're looking for food," Tierza called after her, "you won't find any that you would like."

Odie's tail drooped. Then she straightened it up again proudly. "Says you," she spat, in an unsuccessful attempt to hide her disappointment. She sat down, her ears flattened. She panted a little with exhaustion.

"Well, not just me," Tierza said apologetically. "This is the Royal stable, after all. His Majesty wouldn't allow fish meal or fish in here, nor would Her Royal Highness, for that matter."

"They around?" Odie asked casually. "Princess Arianna and the Sunchaser?"

"Around?" Tierza opened her eyes. "Of course they're around. We've defeated the Shifter and his Shadow army. Her Royal Highness has resumed the throne of Balinor. His Majesty, the Sunchaser, even now walks the Palace grounds. Where have you been, little one, not to know these things?"

"Oh. Here and there. And my name's ODIE!" she shouted. "Not little one." Odie padded back toward Tierza's stall. "Of course I've heard about the victory. Who hasn't? I thought with the celebrations and all, I might come down and see about a job. They say there's jobs here."

"Jobs? What sort of jobs?"

9

"Fightin'," Odie said proudly. "I'm the best fighter in the kingdom. Didn't you see me pounce a minute ago?"

"My, my," Tierza said. Odie was good at picking up unspoken messages: The unicorn was trying to sound impressed. Odie knew she didn't look strong enough to fight a dust bunny, much less anything that would fight back. But Tierza didn't comment on that. She said, "There isn't anyone to fight here in the mews. I'm afraid whoever told you there were jobs here was mistaken."

Suddenly, there was a clatter of hooves on marble, a proud bark, and the sound of a girl's voice in the distance. All the unicorns in the mews looked out into the aisle. Beecher shouted, "They're here!" and Tierza whinnied a glad "Welcome!"

Odie's fur stuck out like a porcupine's, and she streaked under Tierza's stall door like a tiny black comet. She hid in the front corner and peered through the space between the bottom of the door and the floor.

The wide double doors at the end of the building opened and full morning light flooded in. The jewels on the Royal unicorns' horns glowed alive with color.

The Sunchaser himself walked down the aisle!

Odie's eyes widened. The Lord of the Animals in Balinor was huge, larger than any of the other Royal unicorns who looked out from their stalls to greet him. His horn was an ebony spear, and his coat, flowing mane, and tail were molten bronze, matching exactly the beautiful hair of the girl who walked at his side: Arianna, Princess of Balinor and Bonded partner to the Sunchaser himself.

Arianna was dressed simply, in a long, dark red skirt, a full white blouse, and a leather vest. A brown pouch swung from her belt. Next to it was the Royal Scepter, symbol of her power.

Arianna's eyes shone turquoise-blue, and she carried herself straight and proud. And beside her — Odie shrank back into the clean straw of Tierza's stall — beside the Princess was a dog! A *big* dog. A collie with a mahogany-and-cream coat and a plumy tail. *That must be Lincoln, the Princess's constant companion,* Odie thought. She had heard of him, but as far as she was concerned, the only good dog was no dog at all.

Odie growled. The Princess stopped and cocked her head a little. "Did you hear something, Chase?" Her voice was confident and clear, like a bell. "It sounded like a bird."

The collie beside her sniffed the air. "Cat," he said briefly. "And it's hurt."

Arianna turned her startlingly blue eyes and searched the ranks of the unicorns. The Sunchaser raised his muzzle. "Cat," he agreed, his voice a rich rumble of sound. He stepped in front of Arianna protectively. "And there's something odd about it."

"Odd," Odie muttered. "Huh!"

11

"She's here, Your Royal Highness," Tierza said. "Crouched in my stall." She bent her head, and her silky mane flowed around Odie like a sweetly scented curtain. "Don't be afraid, Odie."

"Me? I'm not afraid of nothing!" Odie said with as much belligerence as she could muster. She stood up bravely and stalked into the aisle. She sat down, curled her tail around her feet, and announced for all to hear, "Well, here I am, Your Royal Highness. I came to apply for a job. Odie's my name and fightin's my game. I'm the best fighter in the kingdom!"

Arianna picked up the kitten. Her hands were warm, strong, and reassuring. The cat's nose twitched; the Princess smelled of the outdoors, clean air, and wood smoke.

"You won't have to fight here," Arianna said gently. "Now, what have you been getting into, little one?" Her long fingers caressed Odie's ears. "You've had a hard road, wherever you've been."

Odie tried not to shiver at the Princess's touch. She reminded herself that she *was* the best fighter in the land, and a mighty warrior on top of that, even if she was small and a little scrawny. So if anyone was fit to be held by Her Royal Highness, it was herself — Odie of Ardit.

She growled fiercely and waited for what would come.

3

Arianna cradled the cat with one hand and tried not to laugh at the birdlike growls. The poor thing was so thin! And who had hurt her like this? She reached into the pouch at her belt. Ari's beloved Dr. Bohnes had given her a bag of small magics for such occasions as these, and she always had it with her. She found the small jar containing the healing unguent and scooped a bit onto her finger. She softly worked the salve into Odie's wounds. Her hands stilled when they encountered the ragged collar.

With a frown, she slipped the rags from the cat's neck. The material felt strangely cold and slimy, like raw eggs. Ari tucked the collar into her pouch and covered the rest of Odie's wounds with the salve. Then she closed her eyes and went into the place in her mind where she held her personal magic. Recently, she had had a lot of practice doing this, tending to the wounded from the battle for Balinor.

Around her, the Royal unicorns watched with glowing eyes. Ari concentrated on making the salve heal Odie's cuts and scrapes. A shimmer of blue light enveloped her hands and the cat. A low humming filled the air as the magic salve did its work. Then the light died and sound silenced.

"There," Ari said. She set Odie on the floor and stood up. The little cat sat up and opened her eyes. Her ribs were still visible beneath her black fur, and there were bare spots on her coat where the cruel scratches had been. But the wounds were healed.

"Hey!" Odie said. "I feel pretty terrific — not!" she added with a fierce look at the animals watching her. "Not that I wasn't feeling in fightin' trim before, mind you. But I feel even better now! Bring 'em on!"

"There isn't anyone to fight in the granary," Lincoln said, in a way that implied he'd been insulted. "I made sure of that!"

"Dogs!" Odie sniffed. "What do dogs know about fightin'?"

Lincoln lowered his head and flattened his ears. "Cats!" he growled back. "I've never known a cat who didn't think he should run the entire universe. I've never met a cat who didn't act like a stuck-up . . ."

Ari raised her hand. If she didn't stop this, there was going to be a row. "Enough, enough! Linc,

14

would you go and ask Mrs. Samlett for some milk and fish for Odie?"

"Me? Run an errand for a cat? I was going to the tack room with you and Chase," Lincoln said sulkily. "You were going to put his bridle on Chase to see if Finn had fixed it properly after it broke in the battle with the Shifter. We were also going to plan what to do with all the prisoners of war, then go over those bills Lori ran up when she was swanking around being your lady-in-waiting, and then we were going to —"

"Stop." Ari tapped Lincoln's long nose with one finger. "We'll meet you in the tack room." She stopped and scooped up Odie. "This little thing needs a full stomach before we start the day."

"All right." Lincoln shook himself vigorously. *Probably,* Ari thought with an inward grin, *to rid himself of any lingering scent of cat.* And then he walked off to find Mrs. Samlett.

On their way to the tack room, Ari and Chase stopped to greet each of the Royal unicorns with a word or a pat on the muzzle. The Royals had acquitted themselves nobly in the battle to defeat the Shifter, as had all the people and animals of Balinor. The battle had ended with the arrival of Atalanta, Dreamspeaker to the unicorns of the Celestial Valley and guardian of all of Balinor. Ari would never forget the splendid sight of the Celestial unicorns coming down the Crystal Arch from the Celestial Valley above. She saw them again in her mind's eye as she walked the marble aisle of the mews: glorious, their horns like mighty spears, to defeat the evil Shifter.

And it is not over yet, milady! Chase's voice was in her mind, in the secret language they shared. She glanced at him as he walked beside her. His dark brown eyes were grave.

I know, she thought back to him. She sighed. The Shifter was gone. Balinor was at peace. But she had another task, the most important one of all. When the Shifter conquered Balinor, he had kidnapped her mother and father. Her brothers, too, had disappeared. With the Shifter defeated and her people safe, she now had to find her family and bring them home.

She cuddled Odie under her chin and thought about the collar she'd removed from the cat's neck while healing her. Suddenly, she knew there was a message wrapped in the collar. She had almost known it from the first moment she'd picked up the cat. Ari was in full possession of her own personal magic now, and she understood things she had never before understood.

With her own eyes, she had seen the fall of the Shifter. And as soon as their terrible leader was gone, the Shadow unicorns and the leather-clad soldiers who rode them had given up in defeat and despair.

She *knew* the Shifter was gone forever.

So what was in the message the little cat carried around its neck?

And why did she know the words in it spoke of danger?

Ari worried about this as they left the mews and went into the tack room. Her heart lifted a little. She loved the way the room smelled of well-polished leather and the grit used to clean silver and bronze. The tack room was large, with racks for a hundred unicorn saddles and bridles lining the smooth wood walls. Wide cedar chests filled with saddle blankets and ornamental headdresses for ceremonial occasions divided the flagstone floor down the middle.

Finn, the red-haired captain of the Royal Calvary, was carefully rolling a pair of silk-braided reins as Ari and Chase came in. His face lit up with happiness.

"Your Royal Highness! Your Majesty!" He bowed low. His face bore the marks of the battle the day before: A red weal ran across his forehead, a bruise glowered on his cheek, and he had a terrible-looking black eye. Ari knew these wounds were all testaments to his bravery in the battle against the Shifter and his Shadow army.

Ari smiled at him. "You know better than to 'Royal Highness' me, Finn!"

He straightened up with a grin. "But you really are Her Royal Highness now. We won, Ari! We *won*! I can't believe the Shifter's gone. Forever!"

Ari closed her eyes for a quick moment. "If it hadn't been for you, Chase and I would have been too late to save Balinor." She blinked, then set the little cat on top of one of the cedar chests. "You were wonderful, Finn. You, Rednal, and Toby kept the Shadow unicorns from the Palace walls just long enough for me to come over the hill and call on the Dreamspeaker for help."

Finn's hazel eyes held a faraway expression. "That was a sight I will never forget," he said simply. "To think that I saw Atalanta and the Celestial unicorns!" Then he said quietly, "Too bad that Rednal and Toby had to return to the Celestial Valley."

Ari looked at Finn sympathetically. Atalanta had sent the two Celestial unicorns to Balinor to aid their fight against the Shifter's evil. Finn and Rednal had become very close. At the end of the final battle, Rednal and Tobiano had walked the Crystal Arch behind the Dreamspeaker and returned to their home.

"They had to go back," Chase said gravely. "Celestial unicorns lose their immortality here in Balinor."

"But what about you?" Finn bit his lip, clearly embarrassed at having asked such a personal question of the Sunchaser. The great bronze unicorn was the Lord of the Animals in Balinor, and unlike his mistress, the Sunchaser had never encouraged others to address him in a familiar way. Only Arianna could call him Chase.

"What do you mean, Finn?" Ari leaned over and tickled Odie under her chin. The little cat purred loudly.

"Well, isn't His Majesty a Celestial unicorn?"

"Chase? Of course."

"So he doesn't have his immortality here in Balinor. And he could have been . . ."

"Killed in battle?" Ari said soberly. "Yes." She reached up and ruffled Chase's silky mane. "Yes, he could have been."

"Then it is all for love of you," Finn said, "that he stays here with us."

"Yes," Ari said, a little sadly. "It is the price of the Bond between us."

"I would appreciate it if you wouldn't talk about me as if I weren't in the room," Chase rumbled. "And what I do, I do of my own free will. Now, what about this cat?"

"What *about* that cat?" Finn said. He walked over to the chest and bent over it. "Wow. It looks like it's been in some tough places."

"No tougher than I can handle," Odie swaggered. The swagger would have been much more effective if she hadn't fallen off the chest with a squeak. She shook herself and climbed back on top, then began to groom her tail as if nothing had happened.

"That cat looks half starved," Finn said.

"Which is the only reason I'm waiting on it," Lincoln grumbled around the basket handle in his mouth as he came in. The big collie trotted up to Ari and dropped it with a thump at her feet. "Fish," he said briefly. "And none too fresh." He wrinkled his long nose. "Mrs. Samlett said she was sorry, but there's been no time to reprovision since the battle. There should be a delivery later this morning if you want to wait."

Odie jumped onto the basket and pawed eagerly at the cloth covering her breakfast. Ari pulled the napkin away from the top and looked dubiously at the piece of salmon. Odie darted under her hand and started to gobble. "It's good!" she assured Ari through bits of fish. "I like it this way!"

"If she's used to two-day-old fish, it means she's probably been scavenging most of her life," Chase murmured. "Milady? Perhaps you should read the message in her collar. We may have much to discover about this little cat."

So you know there is danger, too, Ari thought at him.

Chase nodded gravely. *Yes. But first . . .* He then spoke aloud. "Finn?"

"Your Majesty?"

"Have you checked on the prisoners this morning? The soldiers of the Shifter's army are all locked safely away?"

"Yes, Your Majesty. I not only spoke with our guards, but I counted the soldiers myself. They are all present and accounted for. And Mrs. Samlett has seen to it that they are getting a large breakfast of oatmeal and honey." He laughed a little. "I don't think they're too anxious to go back to the Valley of Fear."

"What about Lady Kylie?"

Finn snorted. Everyone hated and despised the snakewoman, emissary of the Shifter and a traitor three times over. *"That* one! She's in the tower and already screeching about her right to a fair trial and the fact that she hates oatmeal. I don't know what she's complaining about — she's got a nicer room in the tower than half the villagers do in their homes."

"How are the wounded?" Chase asked. "And the Shadow unicorns? Still no trace of them?"

Finn's expression was calm and capable. He took his duties seriously. Although he was not much older than Ari herself, his defense of the Palace had been expert, and very few animals or villagers had been wounded. "After the visit you and Ari made to the hospital last night, there are almost no wounded left. There were very few people and animals Her Royal Highness couldn't heal. As for the Shadow unicorns, I sent patrols out all night and again this morning. Same story as last night: No one has seen them since the end of the battle."

There was a worried furrow between Chase's eyes. He took four long strides to the open door and stood gazing out for a moment. He came back to Ari's side, his worry even more pronounced. "I don't like this. I didn't like it last night, and I don't like it now. The Shadow unicorns are creatures of the herd and loyal to their riders. All unicorns are. Even those who have chosen the side of evil. If they abandoned

21

the field and their riders —"He bent his head, deep in thought. Then he said, "There is dark work afoot!"

"What is it?" Ari asked. "What kind of dark work?"

Chase looked at her. *You have a message in your pouch,* he thought-spoke to Ari. *I am afraid that we will now discover just what kind of dark work it is.*

Ari drew out the pouch and clutched the ragged collar. It felt cold and slimy. She opened her hand and looked carefully at the twisted circle of rope and cloth. She knelt on the floor and set the collar down. Finn crouched beside her as she untied the knot that held the ends together.

The collar unfolded itself, like a snake uncoiling from a nap. The rope unraveled and revealed a tightly rolled piece of parchment. Ari could feel the cold coming from it in waves.

Finn gave a startled cry and put his hand out, shielding her. They all stared at it.

It was a plain piece of paper, unmarked, except for the words scrawled in black:

HE MUST BE STOPPED.

4

W ho must be stopped?!" Finn blurted. He reached for the parchment.

"Don't touch it, Finn," Chase warned. "Ari, be careful."

"Where did this come from?" Ari said, more curious than frightened. "And who sent it?" Frowning, she gazed at the message.

Odie, her tummy full of fish, leaped onto Ari's shoulder and stared down at it. "It was very heavy around my neck," she offered. "The man who put it on me said he was sorry. He was a friend, he said, and he was sorry about the message bein' cold. It was *very* cold. I'm glad it's off my neck."

"Who put it on you?" Ari asked softly. Odie's claws tightened. Ari winced and gently pulled them away from her shoulder.

"Sorry," Odie said. "Who put it on me? A man."

"A man?" Ari said. "What man?"

"The same man who told me there would be a job here," Odie said. She began to walk across Ari's shoulders, her tail tickling Ari's ears. "I was checking out the back of a tavern in Sixton three days ago. I was looking for some tasty fish."

"Like the fish you just had?" Lincoln asked.

"Not that good. Anyway, this man in a dusty brown cloak kinda sneaks around the corner of the tavern, like this." Odie leaped to the floor and slunk around Ari's ankles, her eyes narrowed. With her patchy fur sticking up behind her ears and scrawny flanks, she looked both comical and pitiful. "So he sneaks and he sneaks and he comes after me — like this!" She pounced. "And me? I roared back at him, like a lion! I clawed his ankles. I bit his finger! I scratched his face!"

"Oh, for goodness' sake!" Lincoln barked in exasperation. "What a load of fish meal! You didn't do any such thing. Look at you! You obviously lost that fight. Just tell us what happened!"

"He gave me some fish. It distracted me. Otherwise he never would have caught me! I'm not only the best fighter in this kingdom, I'm the finest cat warrior in the whole world!"

Lincoln flopped onto the flagstone and covered his eyes with his paws. "Blabber," he muttered, "blabber, blabber . . ."

"Enough!" Chase's voice was stern.

Odie rolled over on her back in apology. She

looked up at Chase and said meekly, "The man put the collar on me and told me to go to the Royal stables, to see about a job. I don't know who he was, Your Majesty. I ran and ran after he wrapped it around my neck. There was a cart coming this way and I hopped on it and the driver dropped me off in the village. I arrived just after the big battle," she added regretfully. "I would have liked to have seen it. I would have pounced on the Shifter myself!" She began to groom her tail. "That's all I know."

The great unicorn seemed to smile. "That's all you know? Nonsense. You know more than that, Odie. Use the senses the One Who Rules Us All gave animals. What did he smell like? What did the air around him taste like? Where had he been?"

"There was a leaf-mold smell around his feet," Odie said. "And his hands were rough, like a woodchopper's. The air around him smelled like water."

"Leaf mold and fresh water," Finn said. "Could this man have come from the Forest of Ardit? It's a short way from the tavern Odie spoke of to the forest. I know the place."

"I may have an easier way to find out." Ari drew the Royal Scepter from the folds of her skirt and held it up. The Scepter was a beautiful piece of magic: The shaft was made of rosewood heavily inlaid with lapis lazuli. A carved unicorn head with jeweled eyes was fixed to the top. Finn and Lincoln backed away in respect as Ari spoke to the Scepter.

"We have a mysterious message here, Scepter. Can you tell us what it means?"

The rosewood took on the warm glow that meant the Scepter was ready for magic. The unicorn head blinked once or twice and said crossly, "It reads, 'He must be stopped.'"

The Scepter was notorious for both its irritable temper and habit of restating the obvious, so Ari didn't even bother to get annoyed. She was just glad the Scepter responded at all. Sometimes when she asked it questions, the Scepter refused to wake up or said things like "Think it out for yourself." On the other hand, sometimes it was the most powerful magic talisman in Balinor and all the lands beyond. The Scepter was a channel for the Deep Magic, and everyone knew the Deep Magic was a law unto itself.

"But who is *he*?" Ari asked firmly.

Silence.

She tried again. "Who wrote the letter?"

"It's about the Archivist," the Scepter said.

"Who is the Archivist?"

"He works for you, Arianna!" the Scepter said. "Rather, I should say, he works for the Royal family. He is the keeper of your history — all your family's documents and letters and records that date back hundreds and hundreds of years."

"Why, of course!" Ari blinked in surprise. She'd forgotten all about the Archivist, but she remembered him now, in that vague way you remember a distant aunt or uncle who only comes for family parties once a year. "He used to live in the West Tower. And he was in charge of a huge library. Hundreds of scrolls and boxes of musty paper. I visited him once or twice when I was little, I think. His name is Archon."

"Correct," the Scepter said. "When the Shifter took over the Palace on the day of the Great Betrayal, Archon took off with a cart full of your family's documents, as many as he could save."

"Can Archon tell us what this letter means?"

"Probably," the Scepter answered sarcastically, "since he sent the man who wrote the message."

"Was it Archon who gave the message to Odie?"

"That was Archon's friend."

Ari tried another question. "Do you know where Archon is?"

The Scepter didn't answer this right away, but Ari knew it was thinking. Then it said, "Yes. Yes, I do," and then fell into an obstinate silence.

Finn made an exasperated noise and whispered, "Why won't it just *tell* us?"

Ari shook her head slightly. "I'm not sure. But Atalanta once said there are no simple answers. And I know this about the Deep Magic. It has its own logic, which no human or animal can really control. We can only try to direct it. Which makes asking the right questions really hard." She raised her voice a little. "Scepter? Do I need to find the Archivist?"

"Yes." The response was so prompt, Ari knew she was on the right track.

"Do I need to find him quickly?"

"I don't want *you* to find him at all. It isn't safe."

"What will happen if I don't find him?"

"Your parents, the King and Queen, will remain lost forever. Your brothers, the Princes, will never again see the light of day, but live in the darkest place. Shadows will rise over Balinor and you will lose your throne. There is danger."

Ari's heart pounded. "Why?" she demanded. She felt faint with sudden fear. Chase sensed her dizziness and moved to her side. She leaned back and rested a moment against his warm flank. Linc whined worriedly. The silence in the tack room was grave.

"What danger?" Ari said when the dizzy feeling had passed. She forced out the words. "What shadows? Is it the Shifter? It can't be! The Shifter's gone! We all saw what happened! The Dreamspeaker herself was there, I mean, we won the battle. And Balinor is free!"

The Scepter didn't answer for a moment. Then it said slowly, "Shadows. All I see are shadows. And no, it is not the Shifter. He has been sent back to the pits from which he came." The Scepter paused. "I can't answer you anymore, Your Royal Highness. I refuse to be responsible for sending you into danger. Take my advice and stay home."

"When my parents are lost?" Ari asked. "When there are shadows over Balinor? I can't stand by and let doom overtake us!"

"She's right," Finn said, his face pale.

Chase said nothing, but his ears were pricked forward and his whole attention was on his mistress.

"We must visit the tavern where Odie was captured by the man who put the collar around her neck," Ari said slowly. "And then we must find the Archivist." She rubbed Odie's ears to get the cat's attention. "Was this man very old, Odie? Did he have a wispy white beard and very thick eyeglasses?"

"No," Odie said. "He wore a big cloak and he had a hood pulled over his head."

"Then how do you know he didn't have a white beard and wear eyeglasses?" Lincoln demanded.

"I just know," the cat said stubbornly. "He was tall one second and short and squat the next. He changed shape, sort of."

Ari kept her voice steady. "You're sure it wasn't the Shifter?"

"Oh, no. It wasn't. I met the Shifter once," Odie said casually. "In person."

"Oh, you did not!" Lincoln exclaimed. "What a boaster you are!"

"I did! I did! He and his troops were on their way to the Valley of Fear! He smelled like smoke and burning wood."

"And you walked right up to him," Lincoln said. "Sure you did!"

"Nobody walked right up to the Shifter," Odie said sulkily. "Everyone ran away. But I smelled him. And this man didn't smell like that at all." Odie shivered. "This man was cold. *Cold.* I've never felt anything like that before in my life."

"I wonder . . ." Ari said softly.

If the Scepter wasn't going to help, she was just going to have to try on her own. She knelt and flattened the parchment on the flagstone floor, waving away Chase's snort of concern. There was a puzzle here, and she was going to have to use her own magic to solve it. Frequently, the small magic given to her by Dr. Bohnes gave her a big clue.

She shook the contents of her pouch into her hand. The only thing she could be absolutely sure of finding in the magic pouch was Atalanta's Star Bottle, given to her when she and Chase had to go into the terrible Valley of Fear. All the other magics were from Dr. Bohnes. And the contents changed all by themselves. Today there had been the salve for the cat's wounds. But now that had disappeared, and in its place was a glass bottle of powder. The label read: VISIBILITY SALTS (USE ONCE).

Ari picked the bottle up and held it against the light. The powder was the color of cream. Tiny lights flickered in it. Finn leaned over her shoulder and commented, "What good is that? There isn't anything invisible here, is there?"

"How would you know?" the Scepter snapped. "If it's invisible, you can't see it."

Ari closed her hand over the Scepter's head. Sometimes this was the only way to keep the Scepter quiet. She thought for a moment. She had a pretty good idea of how to use the Visibility Salts, but she had to be sure. Dr. Bohnes's bag only allowed one use of each small magic, and what Ari was about to do was too important to risk waste.

The Scepter had a mind of its own, but there was one magical task it always had to perform, no matter what. If Ari asked the Scepter a direct question, requiring a yes or no answer, it had to reply. "Do I shake the salts onto the message, Scepter?"

The Scepter muttered to itself. Ari held the rosewood shaft and looked the unicorn head straight in the eye. "You answer me," she said firmly.

"YES!" the Scepter shouted. "Yes, yes, yes, but don't blame me for what's going to happen!"

Carefully, Ari unscrewed the lid and shook the contents of the bottle over the message. The salts hovered in a sparkling cloud before they settled onto the paper. They billowed and rolled in a wave, obscuring the black ink until they completely covered the words. Then the sparkling lights died away, and Ari could see that the paper was covered with lines. Gently, she blew the salts away and the paper rolled up with a snap.

"It's a map!" Finn said. He bent over and

smoothed the map open. "Well, part of a map, anyway. It's also partly blank."

"It shows the southern part of Balinor," Ari said. "There's Blue Mountain, the Sixth Sea, and the Port of Sixton. Why, even the entrance to the Gap is marked. It's in the middle of the Valley of Fear. Except the Valley of Fear isn't there anymore. It just says TERRA INCOGNITA. And Demonview has a new name, too."

"Shadowview," Finn read.

The fresh morning light seemed to dim. A cold breeze swept through the tack room as Finn pronounced the name.

"There's a spell at the bottom of the map," Chase said. "Do you see?"

"How do you know it's a spell?" Lincoln asked.

"Because it says so," Ari explained. It always puzzled her that Lincoln couldn't read. Every other animal in Balinor could. Perhaps the fact that Lincoln was from beyond the Gap explained it. She pushed the thought away. This wasn't the time to think about the Gap. Not now. If she thought about the Gap, she'd have to think about Lori Carmichael and how to get her home. Now Ari's lady-in-waiting, Lori had followed Ari and Linc when they had tumbled through the Gap into Balinor.

"There just isn't any time," she said in frustration. "But it is a spell, Lincoln. See?" She pointed to it. It was written in a thick scarlet ink, totally different from the black words HE MUST BE STOPPED, which were now at the top of the partial map of southern Balinor.

"It says this," Finn said. And he read,

"A Spell for the Traveler:
Set aside the robes of state,
The Crown, the Throne, the Wand of Fate.
Remain disguised in look and sound
To find the one who must be found."

The map rolled itself up again, as if reluctant to be read.

"But where would we go?" Ari wondered. "And what exactly are we looking for?"

"The Archivist," Finn said promptly. "According to the Scepter, at least."

"The man in the cloak?" Lincoln suggested. "He delivered the message, after all. If we find him, he may know where the Archivist is."

"The man in the cloak probably came from the Forest of Ardit," Finn said.

Lincoln wagged his tail slowly. "If we can believe that cat."

"Cats don't lie!" Odie said indignantly. They all looked at her. "Well, we don't. We lurk. We pounce. Once in a while we sneak. But we don't lie."

"I know cats don't lie," Ari said soothingly. "But I wish we knew what it is we're supposed to do. He must be stopped. *He must be stopped.*" She repeated the words as if they themselves would provide a clue to the destination of their journey. She unrolled the map again and concentrated.

"I didn't see this before. It's hard to see because it's in the shaded area of Shadowview. But look, Chase."

Chase bent his head. His horn touched her arm gently. "It's a comet," he said in a puzzled voice. "A tiny comet." He bent closer, and the tip of his horn brushed the infinitesimal shape. Suddenly, the comet flared yellow-green, a burst of light like a soundless firecracker. Everyone jumped back.

"Did you see what happened?" Finn demanded in excitement. "When the comet flared, the rest of the map showed up!"

"The rest of the map?" Ari asked, bewildered.

"Yes! It's gone now, but all the space that's marked Terra Incognita — where the Valley of Fear used to be — filled up with hills and valleys and roads and . . . It was too fast to really see it all," he added apologetically.

"The burst of light made you see things?" Lincoln asked skeptically. "I didn't see anything more than I saw before. Blank spots. That's all. Just blank spots."

Finn shook his head. "I know what I saw."

"Maybe we have to go to the spot where the comet is to find out where we go from there," Ari said slowly. "Wait. I'll ask the Scepter. Do we go to the spot where the comet is? The place that's halfway up Shadowview?"

The Scepter said, "Yes," in a tight, clipped voice that meant its patience was truly being tried.

"And then what?" Ari encouraged.

"Stay home," the Scepter said. "Just stay home. Let events take their course without you."

"No," Ari said. "We're not staying home." She looked at the others. "So that's our destination. Shadowview. I suppose we will find out more when we get there."

No one answered her. Not even Chase.

Finn was the one who said, "So, it looks like we're taking another trip!" He grinned happily. He loved adventure. "Onward!"

5

"You cannot leave now, Your Royal Highness!" Lord Artos fairly bounced on his chair. One of the three lords of the Royal Council, Artos was short and bouncy, like a rubber ball.

Ari shook her head regretfully. "I must, milord." She had called a Council meeting as soon as she'd realized Finn was right: She and Chase had to search for the Archivist so that he could tell them who must be stopped, and why. They had to leave Balinor at once. She glanced out the long floor-to-ceiling window that lined the hall; it was already midmorning, and she had much to do before she could set out on her journey.

Council meetings were held in the Great Hall, a long, marble-floored room in the center of the Palace. Yesterday, the room had been filled with villagers and knights who had fought the Shifter. Although Mrs. Samlett had done her best to tidy up, the room was littered with cloaks, broken

36

swords, a battered shield or two, and other items left behind when the Palace army had gone home.

Ari and the lords of the Council were seated at the long wooden table set in front of the thrones of Balinor. She had taken an oath not to sit on the throne until her family returned, and she sat at the end of the table, facing Lords Puckenstew, Artos, and Rexel. Chase and Finn stood behind her and Lincoln was at her feet. Odie had skittered under the table when the lords assembled. She hid under Ari's long skirt, and Ari could feel the little cat curled against her ankle.

"I'm afraid I have no choice," Ari said.

"And you won't tell us why?" Lord Rexel stroked his chin. He was tall and very thin. Although he and his knights had fought well the day before, it was hard for Ari to like him. He was always so grim. And his knights always looked as if they didn't get enough to eat.

"It's Royal business," Chase said shortly. "We will leave the kingdom in the Council's hands, milord. We will return as soon as we can."

"But you've just returned, Princess!" Lord Puckenstew, the third member of the Council, was huge, muscular, and strong as an ox. Ari liked Puckenstew a great deal; he was a former knight of her father's and a very kind man. "We were planning a huge celebration in the village. The people of Balinor want to see you. And the animals are all eager to see His Majesty again!"

"So what's going on?" Lori Carmichael marched determinedly into the room and sat down next to Ari without so much as a bow.

Lord Rexel looked disapproving.

Lord Puckenstew cleared his throat with a marked "humph!"

Lord Artos scowled.

Lori blinked innocently at the lords.

Ari noticed right away that Lori was wearing yet another new gown. She had named Lori as one of her ladies-in-waiting at the insistence of the lords, who were very fussy about Royal protocol. Ari had regretted the decision the moment she'd agreed; she didn't need a lady-in-waiting. The only good thing about it was that being a lady-in-waiting kept Lori out of Ari's hair.

Lori was Ari's age, with thick blond hair and a fresh complexion. Like Lincoln, Lori wasn't really from Balinor, but from beyond the Gap, the place where Atalanta had hidden Ari and Chase when the Shifter had ruled Balinor. Lori had come to Balinor by accident. And had managed to stay there ever since.

"You're supposed to bow in the presence of Her Royal Highness," Finn said properly.

Lori smirked. "We know each other too well for that, don't we, Ari, old pal? And you should address *me* as Lady Lori, Finn."

38

Ari rapped the table lightly with her knuckles to get everyone's attention. "Finn, Chase, Lincoln, and I will leave tonight," she said. "We hope to return soon. But we really can't give you a definite time. We will send messages when we —"

"Wait — wait — wait," Lori said, breaking yet another rule of Royal etiquette by interrupting Ari. "You guys are leaving? Now? There's supposed to be this huge party in the village to celebrate our victory. I ordered a new dress and everything."

Ari wound a strand of her hair around one finger and tugged at it thoughtfully. The map showed an entrance to the Gap. Lori had been in Balinor far past the time when she should have returned to Glacier River Farm. Although time was different there — only a few hours had passed on the other side of the Gap while months had passed in Balinor — Lori had to get home before she was seriously missed by her parents.

Now that she was in full possession of her magic, Ari could send Lori home, where she belonged. And besides, that could give the curious lords a good reason why she had to leave now, at a time when she should be taking up the duties of the kingdom. *What do you think?* she thought at Chase. *Is Lori's return to Glacier River a sufficient excuse for our absence?*

I would prefer that we not tell anyone where we are going, Chase thought back to Ari. *I am uneasy. I trust no one but ourselves, milady. There may be enemies anywhere. So, yes, tell the lords we are taking Lori home. But don't tell them the location of the entrance to the Gap.*

Ari sighed. This was the hard part of being a Princess. Her parents had lost the throne through treachery — could she and Chase be sure of anyone but themselves until her mother and father returned?

"We must take you home, Lori," she said gently. "It is past time for you to return."

"This is the reason you are leaving now?" Lord Rexel demanded. "To take her to the Gap? You don't owe her a thing, Your Royal Highness. She should not be a reason to abandon the affairs of state!"

Lori sat up with a snort. Ari held her hands up for silence. There were good things about being a Princess, too. And this was one of them. "That's enough," she said quietly. "I have spoken. Chase and I will leave tonight. We will take Finn and Lori with us."

"Yes, Your Royal Highness," Lord Rexel said.

"Very well, Your Royal Highness." Lord Puckenstew bowed.

"I'll miss you, Princess!" Lord Artos shook his head. "But we will do our best to take care of matters here while you are gone. Yes, we will do our best!"

Odie climbed into Ari's lap and began to purr.

"I don't want to go home!" Lori wailed later that afternoon.

Mrs. Samlett shook her head in an exasperated way and looked at Ari. "And indeed, Princess, I don't know why *you* should be the one to journey all the way to the Gap. Let Master Finn do it!"

Ari hugged Runetta affectionately. All three of them — Ari, Lori, and Mrs. Samlett — were in Ari's bedroom at the Palace. Mrs. Samlett insisted on packing for Ari and shook her head in dismay when Ari told her to put only warm boots, cloaks, and plain jerkins in her knapsack.

Runetta Samlett and her husband had been Ari and Chase's loyal supporters all through the battles against the Shifter. But Ari couldn't even tell the loyal Innkeepers the true nature of her quest. The rosy-cheeked woman was quite unhappy at the thought of her Princess sleeping outdoors at night, away from the luxury of the Palace.

"And you're not taking any Royal robes with you?" she cried. "Why don't you go in the Royal coach? With enough servants to help you camp out in style?"

"It's just for a few days," Ari soothed her. "And we need the Royal Scepter to get through the Gap, Runetta, so Finn can't possibly go by himself. And we're all in disguise because —" She thought rapidly. "Because we don't want to be delayed by stopping to greet people when we travel. You know how it is, if people hear that the Royal coach is coming, they'll want to have a feast, they'll want to get all dressed up for a Royal event, and it'll take far too

41

much time. It's much better that Chase and I travel incognito."

"Feasts sound good to me," Lori said sourly. "I like a good feast. And Lady Kylie told me that people give you things when you travel in a Royal procession."

"And what were you doing talking to *that* one," Runetta scolded Lori. "Lady Kylie indeed! I call Kylie a *traitor*, and so does everyone else."

"I don't like her any more than you do," Lori said defensively. "I just went to see her in the tower, that's all. She'd borrowed my diamond diadem and I wanted it back."

"Nothing but trouble, that young miss!" Runetta muttered under her breath. "Meaning Lady Lori, milady. And Kylie, too! Why don't you take that snaky horror and drop *her* into the Gap while you're at it!"

"Kylie will be tried when Chase and I return," Ari said. "I'm ready now, Runetta. I have the Scepter, my pouch from Dr. Bohnes, and three changes of clothes."

Once again, the words of the Traveler's Spell ran through Ari's mind: *Set aside the robes of state.* She looked down at her simple skirt and boots. Would she ever wear the real clothes of a Princess? She bit back a laugh: Did she even want to wear them? She forced herself to pay attention to the task at hand. "Lori? Are you ready, too?"

Lori hefted a huge knapsack off the floor and shoved a large chest with her sandaled foot. "I guess so."

"You can't take all that!" Runetta said, scandalized.

"Why not?" Lori pouted. "It's my lady-in-waiting dresses. The silks, the brocades, the jewels. I'm not leaving them behind!"

"None of it will go through the Gap," Ari said. "I'm afraid you'll have to leave it. All you can take is what you had when we came through. And your clothes."

"All I had was my breeches and boots and shirt. The stuff I have on now so that I don't get all dirty traveling."

"Then that's it, I'm afraid."

"Well, I won't leave my jewels." Lori folded her arms. "I'm not going."

All the way down the stairs and all the way to the mews, where Finn, Lincoln, and Chase were waiting, Lori insisted she wasn't going without her elegant clothes and finery. Tierza and Beecher had volunteered to accompany the traveling party, and the two Royal unicorns were waiting with excited eyes and flared nostrils for the journey to start. Lori stopped whining when she saw Tierza.

"Can I ride her?" she asked as soon as she set eyes on the graceful black unicorn. "She's beautiful," she added breathlessly.

43

"You will have to ask her," Chase said. "But I think it would be best, Tierza, since Beecher and Finn appear to be getting along well."

The lovely unicorn nodded acceptance, and Lori sprang onto her back. Ari fit her saddlebags onto Chase's flanks and mounted. The two of them wheeled to survey the party. Finn was on Beecher, and it was clear that the powerful Royal unicorn and the captain of the Royal Cavalry were going to get along well. Lincoln was brushed and gleaming, ready to start. Next to him was the little cat Odie, a bright red bandanna tied around her neck.

"I figured I might as well come along, too," Odie said in an offhand way. "If you don't mind."

Ari looked at the cat. The map and the collar were a cold weight in her pouch. And the cat had been the messenger. *What do you think, Chase?*

Yes, he thought back. *The cat should go. She knows the messenger, after all. She can ride on your shoulder.*

Ari nodded. Odie leaped to Ari's boot and scrambled up onto Ari's shoulder.

They waved farewell to Runetta and were on their way.

Kylie, the snakewoman, watched them leave from her cell in the Palace tower. It was comfortable, the tower. She had been in worse places. The Shifter's tower, for one, not to mention the miserable Pit.

Those places had been cold and dark and cruel. This place was warm.

The late evening twilight poured through the high window. The view below was beautiful. The green fields of Balinor spread out like a tapestry with figures woven into it: three beautiful unicorns, the bronze-haired Princess, and her dog.

Kylie spat. *Curses!* She was growing soft here in this cell, cut off from her evil friends. There were only mere touches of snake about her now. She was unable to change into reptile form. When the Shifter had been defeated, his dark magic had died with him. But her eyes were still snakelike: dull yellow with vertical black pupils. As she prowled the carpeted floor restlessly, her black hair whipped back and forth, the tendrils like snakes in miniature.

"Fools!" Kylie grasped the iron bars of the window with both hands and rattled them. She stared up at the sky. The sun was setting in a blaze of gold and orange. And faintly — no more than a pale smudge against the glory of the early evening — she saw the tail of a comet.

She grinned happily, exposing her pointed teeth. "You wait! You just wait, you perfect, pretty little Princess Arianna!" She laughed, a peculiar hissing sound that barely split the air. "Kraken is coming!"

6

The visible part of the magic map directed the travelers through familiar territory: the road to Sixton, some eighteen hours away by unicorn. They would stop as deep evening fell, then stop again the next day at the tavern where Odie had met the cloaked man.

Ari kept her own cloak over her head and darkened the distinctive jewel at the base of Chase's horn with lampblack. If anyone asked questions, they would say that they were part of Lord Puckenstew's household, returning to Sixton to visit relatives after the victory over the Shifter. Everywhere they went they saw happy people and even happier animals. The rule of the Shifter was over, and the country of Balinor rejoiced.

The first night, they stopped at a small country Inn four hours away from the Palace. The Innkeeper and her brother were filled with praises for the Princess and His Majesty, the Sunchaser. "For I'll tell you this, miss," the quiet little Innkeeper said to Lori as she cleared away the dishes from supper. "There never was a better day for Balinor than when Her Royal Highness returned!"

"I hear that her lady-in-waiting — Lady Lori, I think her name is — I hear she was important to the victory, too," Lori said.

Lincoln growled a little, low in his throat. Lori glared at him and growled back.

Ari went to her room soon after, carrying Odie with her. The night was warm, and Lincoln, with his heavy coat, said he was going to sleep outside with Chase, where there was at least a chance of a breeze. Ari got ready for bed, already half-asleep. It had been a long few days. And although she had slept well the night before — the sleep of victory — she had gotten to bed late.

Ari welcomed the snug bed here at the Inn, with its soft goose-down mattress and brightly colored summer quilt. She knelt on the mattress and opened the small window to the night air. Odie bounced up beside her and looked out, too.

"No moon," Odie said, staring up at the sky with her big yellow eyes. "What's that up there?" she asked after a moment. "That star with a tail."

Ari rubbed her eyes. "A comet!" she said. "I noticed it last night. It's getting closer, too. It's beautiful, don't you think?"

47

"No. I think something's wrong with it," Odie said in a worried way.

"Now, don't be scared," Ari said kindly. "We don't see comets very often in Balinor, Odie."

"Good," Odie replied.

Ari smiled. "Let's get some sleep."

She fell gratefully onto the bed and into a deep sleep.

Odie curled beside her, her cat's eyes fixed on the comet. "You are ugly," she said. "Ugly, ugly. That's a creepy light you've got there, comet. And I can tell because I can see better than any human or unicorn or dog in Balinor." She folded her paws under her chest and resolved to watch and wait all night if need be. The comet was coming closer. And anything that ugly getting close to the Princess was going to have to go through Odie the Great first! The cat lifted her lip in a silent snarl. She'd pounce on that comet if it even came near the window. She'd grab it by the tail!

Odie sniffed. Roses? She smelled roses! And the light in the room was turning the most wonderful violet-blue. The light swirled like water in a whirlpool. And it was forming . . . it was forming a bridge over the bed!

Odie's eyes widened. Something wonderful was coming. Something that blotted out the light of that ugly comet. She squeezed her eyes shut.

"Odie." The voice was kind, gentle, and infinitely sweet. The scent of roses fell about the room like a veil. Odie opened one eye. The light from the stars had come together and made a silver bridge that ended at the foot of the bed where Arianna slept. And on the bridge walked the most beautiful unicorn Odie had ever seen. She was a shimmering violet, with a moon-colored mane and tail. Her mane flowed like a crystal river to her knees, and her tail drifted in the dark like ghostly constellations. And her eyes! Her eyes were the kindest Odie had ever seen: starry purple with an amused twinkle in their depths.

"Well, little Odie. And do you protect the Princess?"

Odie swallowed hard. "You bet I do!" she squeaked. She knew who this must be. She had heard tales of the legendary Atalanta, the Dreamspeaker, guardian of all who lived in Balinor and mate to Numinor, the Golden One. This was her presence, or a dream of it, right here in front of the greatest cat warrior in Balinor! Odie crawled up the blankets to sit near Arianna's shoulder. "D-d-don't come any nearer!" Odie warned. "I'm not really the greatest cat warrior in Balinor," she found herself admitting. It was impossible to fib under the gaze of those celestial eyes. "I'm just a regular cat. But I'll die for the Princess!"

"Do you know me, little one?" Atalanta asked.

"Oh, yes, I do." Odie looked up. "You are the Dreamspeaker. The one who walks the path to the moon."

49

"So you must know I love Arianna and all who live in Balinor."

"Yes, ma'am."

"And I would not harm her. Not for this world or the next."

"No, ma'am."

"Then you must move away from Arianna, Odie. I have a message to send her as she dreams. You cannot interfere with that."

"Well, I wouldn't!" Odie said indignantly. "But . . . but . . . you will be careful?"

"I will indeed, Odie. And you are the bravest cat in Balinor! For I know of none other who would dare to interfere with a visitor from the Celestial Valley." The purple eyes grew thoughtful. "We may need this fearless love of yours, Odie, before events are finished."

The light around the Dreamspeaker swelled to such intensity that Odie closed her eyes again. Ari stirred and murmured. Odie's quick ears caught Atalanta's whispering as she sent her dream abroad to trouble Ari's sleep. "The Wand of Fate, Arianna. You must leave the Wand of Fate behind! If you do not, you will never find the Archivist!"

Odie felt a gentle breath on her ears. "You will forget me, little Odie. But I will not forget you."

The moonlight faded away. The smell of roses vanished. Odie opened her eyes to an ordinary dark. Had someone been here? She couldn't remember. But there was a sweet taste in her mouth, and she was very happy.

She curled up at Ari's feet and fell into a dreamless sleep.

"My goodness, you're sleeping hard!" said Princess Arianna.

Odie woke up with a start. Ari was already out of bed and dressed. She laughed tenderly and gently rubbed the spot beneath Odie's chin, which made the cat purr.

"You did, too!" Odie leaped to the floor and stretched.

"I had a dream, though." Ari frowned thoughtfully. "Odie? Did you hear anything in the night?"

Odie blinked at her. Ari rubbed her forehead. There was something she had to do. "Odie, will you scoot down and make sure that Lori and Finn will be ready to go soon? I'd like to reach Sixton as soon as we can today."

Odie nodded vigorously. "I'm the best cat messenger in Balinor," she said. "I'll get everyone up, even if I have to scratch 'em and scratch 'em."

"Well, don't do that. But see that they hurry along." Odie scampered out of the room. Ari heard the soft tap of the little cat's paws on the wooden stairs. She held the Royal Scepter in one hand and looked at it doubtfully.

"Atalanta came to me. I'm certain of it. The

spell," she murmured. "I was in such a rush to leave Balinor and find the Archivist that I forgot about the spell. We are all in disguise — but that isn't enough. I have to leave the wand of fate. And that's you, isn't it, Scepter?"

The Scepter blinked to life and uttered a disconsolate "yes."

"I should have locked you in the Treasury," Ari said.

"You shouldn't put me anywhere! We should all go home!"

"You know I can't."

"I knew this would happen. I *knew* this would happen. I'm not going to be around to help you, Princess. And you are headed into more danger than you know." Because the unicorn head was wooden, it couldn't really gnash its teeth, but it was very frustrated. Ari could see that. "I'm not supposed to get involved," the Scepter said crossly. "I'm supposed to be a force for the general good — not a champion of the individual. But I can't help myself, Princess. I'm becoming very attached to you."

"Well, thank you. I guess."

"Don't thank me! If I don't remain a detached and uninvolved symbol of the Deep Magic, the Old One will yank my powers quicker than you can say 'scat!' "

"You mean the Old Mare of the Mountain?" Ari asked. She had met the Old Mare several times in her adventures in Balinor. The Old Mare had powers beyond even the Dreamspeaker's, beyond any magic that Ari had encountered anywhere else. And the Scepter was right: The Deep Magic was a force. If an evil being like the Shifter used it, it could be directed for evil. The Dreamspeaker used it for good, as did Ari herself, she hoped. But the Deep Magic didn't take sides. It couldn't. Like fire, it could warm you or burn your house down, depending on how careful you were.

Ari considered her options. She took a deep breath. "What if I took you anyway? If I . . ." She swallowed hard. "If I just continued to kind of . . . forget that I was supposed to leave you behind? What would happen then?"

"There are two possibilities," the Scepter said, with all of its old Deep Magic detachment. "The first is: I'd become useless. The second is: You'd become useless. In either case, you would have made a dishonorable decision, and ultimately you'll pay for it."

"But I'm not the only one who's in danger," Ari argued. "There's Lori and Lincoln and Finn and Tierza and Beecher. And above all . . ."

"The Sunchaser."

"Yes." Ari held up the Scepter. "But I know what he would tell me to do." She sighed. She had been counting on the Scepter to help her. "Well, where should I hide you?"

"Bury me," the Scepter said dramatically.

"Bury me in the Forest of Ardit. But do not forget me, Princess Arianna. And when you have done what you must do, don't forget to dig me up again."

The Scepter seemed to frown, although its wooden expression didn't change. "I'll probably rot, being wood," it said gloomily. "And since I shouldn't be with you right now, don't use me, for goodness' sake! Just pretend I'm another piece of wood hanging from your belt."

"It's not as bad as all that," Ari said cheerfully. "Why, I managed without you before, Scepter. And very nicely, too. Things are going to be just fine." She tucked the Scepter into its accustomed place on her belt, her private thoughts not at all as cheerful as her tone.

Ari decided not to announce her decision to leave the Scepter behind on the trip to Terra Incognita until the very moment she had to. Without the protection of the Scepter, Chase would almost certainly want Ari to turn back. He and Finn would insist on completing their quest to find the Archivist — but with a platoon of unicorns and knights at her back! Atalanta had told her there was no time. *No time.* And there was no time to wait for her army.

She gathered her knapsack together, put Odie on her shoulder, and went down to make sure that Chase had his breakfast.

The Inn had several small paddocks outside

the guest barn for visiting unicorns. Chase was in the largest one, cropping grass. Lincoln sat beside him. They were in deep discussion. Lincoln got up and came to greet her, his tail wagging slowly. Ari scratched behind his ears, then unpacked Chase's currycomb and started to groom his sleek coat. Odie prowled restlessly around Ari's shoulders. "So what were you and Lincoln talking about when I walked over?" Ari asked presently.

Chase raised his head to the sky. "That."

"That what?" Ari peered up. The sky was a very pale blue, almost gray. Furry white clouds were gathered on the horizon, a sure sign of rain. Very faintly, she could see the comet. "Oh, yes. I saw it last night. Odie and I were stargazing."

"I was up early this morning," Lincoln said. "There's a small village about half a mile west of here, and I wandered through it. Folks were very disturbed by the comet."

"Oh?" Ari turned to Chase. "It's not that unusual, is it? I've never seen one, but I have heard of such things before."

"I don't know what it means, if anything," Chase agreed. "But sometimes the people get uneasy when something occurs for which there is no easy explanation. I would like to be back in Balinor, milady. We could issue a proclamation from the Palace that this is an unusual occurrence, but not a dangerous one."

55

"Perhaps Lord Puckenstew will do that," Ari said. "I can send him a message. I'm sure there's a unicorn message service in the village."

"He doesn't have the power of the Scepter," Lincoln said. "So the proclamation should be from you, after you ask the Scepter what the comet means. I can fetch some parchment for you to write on, if you like."

Ari bit her lip. Lincoln and Chase watched her, waiting. One last time. She would use the Scepter one last time. What harm could come of that?

7

Agreat crow rode the desolate winds blowing over the lands that had once been the Valley of Fear. There was nothing left here after the Shifter's defeat. Castle Entia lay in ruins; its huge granite blocks lay tumbled this way and that. The courtyard where once the Shadow unicorns had gathered with their leather-clad riders was bare of all but sand. The terrible Pit, where slaves of the Shifter had labored under the hot desert sun, lay empty.

The wind was capricious, blowing sand and thorny branches first one way, then another. The fire that once flamed beneath this terrible place was extinguished, the hot coals that once formed the central pathway through the Valley of Fear mere piles of ash.

The crow sailed the winds like a ship on an uneasy sea. The bird was huge, and occasionally the shadow of his wings swept across the desert with an echo of his old master's power.

There! At the very bottom of the empty Pit! Only a bird's sharp eye could have seen the movement in the soil there. Something . . . something was coming up.

The crow screeched, then dived into the Pit. He circled as he flew deeper and deeper. He landed and shook his wings with a furious rattle of feathers and beak. There was one last magic left to him. One spell that would transform him into his true form: Moloch, lead unicorn of the Shadow herd, chosen steed of the Shadow Rider, who had been the Shifter's chief ally.

Should he use the last spell now? He clawed at the sand where he had seen something trying to burrow up. Now the sand was still; a few grains trickled into a small depression, but that was all.

Moloch stared at the sky. The winds swirled and blew, but yes, he could see it, the comet. The comet that would pull his new master out of the earth. That would free him to rebuild the Valley of Fear. But it was still in the future. Another few days, perhaps.

Perhaps less.

Moloch pushed himself into the air. He could wait. But while he waited, he would do what he could to prepare the way. For nothing must interfere with the rebuilding of the Valley of Fear. He soared high into the air and beat his way toward what had once been the mountain called Demonview.

Beyond the mountain was the Sixth Sea. And

beyond that, Balinor, home of the wretched unicorn who called himself Lord of the Animals. Not to mention that blue-eyed brat, the Princess. If it hadn't been for them —! Moloch gnashed his beak. He would still be herd leader of the Shadow herd. He would still have slaves to serve his every desire.

And now? Now he had nothing.

The crow-shape screamed in fury. Moloch would take his revenge, if he could. But the Princess was guarded, not only by the giant unicorn but by her own personal magic. If he could just find Princess Arianna and that bronze-colored fool, he could do something to impress his new master. *Anything* to impress his new master.

Moloch flew across the Sixth Sea, his eyes fixed on Sixton and the far horizon. Forests covered much of Balinor, and if he was right — he had to be right — he would find them hiding there: his herd, the Shadow unicorns, with eyes like burning coals, horns sharpened to deadly points. He could rally them against Princess Arianna and her kind.

Or better yet! If just once — just once — she left the safety of the Palace without her magic . . . he, Moloch, would find her! And that would be the end of Princess Arianna!

Moloch shrieked again. He flew straight on, past the sea, past Sixton, and on his way to the village of Balinor, where he had last seen the Shadow herd defeated by the hateful Princess and her unicorn. And as he flew, he watched the ground, his keen crow's eyes penetrating the thick trees of the Forest of Ardit, the Forest of Fellows, and all the groves and woods that lay between them. He flew on and on, past farms, villages, and fields.

And almost froze in midair.

Was someone working magic outside of Balinor? Was that the rosy glow of the Royal Scepter? Could it be?

Moloch folded his wings against his body and plummeted headlong to earth.

8

Ari held the Scepter in its usual position and willed it to begin its magic. The rosewood glowed, but dimly.

Milady? Chase's thought was warm, insistent. *You don't seem your usual self. Is anything wrong?* Ari shut her mind against Chase. This was the first time she had ever denied him. She blinked back tears.

She kept her mind shut.

"Milady!" He spoke aloud, the concern in his voice so obvious that Lincoln jumped to his feet and whined in distress. She couldn't look at Chase. He knew her too well. "In a moment, Chase," she said aloud, as coolly as she could. "And let's not use thought-speak, okay? It's really not fair to Lincoln."

The collie's eyes widened in astonishment. Ari felt the hurt coming from Chase in a flood of sorrow and grief. But she couldn't let him know what she was thinking. The Scepter had told her the fate of the throne of Balinor, her parents, and her brothers depended on her discovery of the Archivist. And she couldn't go back for reinforcements. Not now.

Do you wish to break the Bond? The unhappiness in his thought was like a blow.

Ari willed her voice to be steady. "Of course not. Now let's all settle down and let me ask the Scepter about the comet, and we can get on with what we have to do."

A huge black bird circled above their heads, blotting out the weak morning sun. Lincoln barked ferociously at it. The bird cawed mockingly at them, almost as if it knew what was going on. It flew into the trees surrounding the paddock and disappeared.

"Now, Scepter. I have a question."

"Your Royal Highness," the Scepter said. But its voice was faint, the glow of its magic so dim in the pale sunlight, it might not have been working at all.

"Can you give the people of Balinor some reassurance about this comet? We wish to write a proclamation to calm our people."

"We?" Lincoln said. "That's the first time I've ever heard you use the royal 'we,' milady."

"Well, it's the first time I've ever had to write a Royal proclamation," Ari confessed. "I'm not sure how to do it."

"Comet!" said the Scepter weakly. "Do not . . ."

The glow faded and went out. The Scepter was cold in her hands.

If I do, the Old One will stop the Deep Magic, the Scepter had said.

And it looked as if the Old Mare had done precisely that.

"Now what?" Ari said. "Chase?" But the big unicorn had turned his back to her. His head drooped. Even the glorious bronze of his coat looked dull. Ari ran to him and gently caressed his neck. "I'm sorry," she whispered. "I just . . . Chase! Please forgive me. I didn't mean to hurt you."

He nudged her with his muzzle. *I understand.*

She smiled, blinking back tears, and combed a burr out of his forelock. But she still kept her mind closed to him. "We'll have to talk to that nice Innkeeper about weeding her pasture," she scolded gently. "You've never had a burr before. Come on. Let's find the others. I want to get started right away."

Ari wrapped the Scepter in her second-warmest cloak and put it away in Chase's saddlebag. They started off to Sixton, and it was a miserable journey. It began to rain hard, a summer rain with big fat raindrops that soaked them all. Lori was still in a miserable mood, complaining every five seconds about the loss of all her new clothes and jewelry. Chase was stonily silent, carrying Ari with a rigid back and working at a backbone-jarring trot. Odie clung to Ari's shoulder, under her cloak, and kept very quiet. Finn, after a few attempts at conversation, settled into a tuneless whistle that drove Ari quite mad. Lincoln trotted along next to Tierza and Beecher and kept to himself.

It was dark by the time they reached the Port of Sixton. Despite the grim nature of their journey, Ari had been looking forward to seeing the port again. She really liked Captain Tredwell of the *Dawnwalker*, the ship that had carried them over the Sixth Sea to Demonview — when it had been Demonview and not Shadowview, as the magic map called it now.

She'd been hoping that the *Dawnwalker* would be in the harbor and would carry them across the sea to the shores of the mountain. It was a lot quicker to get to the Valley of Fear — no, it wasn't the Valley of Fear anymore, she'd have to learn to call it Terra Incognita!

"Let's stop here," Chase suggested as they came to the main intersection of the town. "We want to visit the tavern where Odie ran into the cloaked man. I believe we must turn down this alley and cut across the old vegetable market."

Ari raised her head and looked around. The cobblestone streets were almost deserted, the rain having driven everyone inside. The only torches that were lit were under the overhangs of the shops. It was far too wet for the outdoor ones. It was very gloomy. "I don't quite see where the alley is," Ari said.

"Right here!" a voice squawked.

A huge crow hopped down from the barrel where it had been perched. Ari jumped. She hadn't seen the crow sitting there. The bird hopped forward on its crooked legs. It cocked its head and regarded them with curiously bright eyes. "Right over here, gentlefolk. Turn down this way. Here! I'll show you!" It flew up with a sudden, almost alarming rush of its coal-black wings.

Ari cued Chase with her knees, and he obediently turned to the left. Lori and Tierza followed right behind them.

Finn and Beecher hung back. "I'll catch up," Finn called. "I just have to fix this stirrup leather."

It was so dark it was hard to see in the alley. The rain came down harder than ever. The cobblestone way was very narrow, and Chase's quarters almost touched the houses on each side. The windows in the houses were darkened; the only light came from a shrouded lantern swinging at the far end of the alley.

"Here!" the crow croaked. "Stop right here!" The crow's eye gleamed bloodred as it caught a stray beam of light.

Chase saw the dark figures first; they appeared out of nowhere, with hoods drawn over their faces. He lunged forward, using his horn as a weapon, and there was a clash of metal, reminiscent of the sounds of the battle with the Shifter's army. The great unicorn reared and tried to back up. He collided with the frantic Tierza, who was lunging forward, too. There was no place to turn! No way to turn.

Lori screamed.

Odie yowled and tried to claw her way free from under Ari's cloak. "Let me at 'em!" she shouted. "Let me *at* 'em!"

Ari drew her battle knife from her boot and gripped it as Chase had taught her: thumb under the hilt, fingers wrapped tightly around the jeweled end of the shaft. A thickset figure jumped up and grabbed Chase by the bit. The unicorn paid no attention to the pain, but shook his head fiercely from side to side. Someone else grabbed Ari's boot and pulled her down. She swung out with the knife, aiming for the gauntlet clawing at the leather.

Lori's screams were so loud, Ari was sure that help would come from the good people of Sixton. She heard the thump of Tierza's frantic kicks against the close-set walls of the alleyway.

A second joined the figure pulling at Ari's boot. She swung the knife again and overbalanced, falling into rough cloth, a heavy chest, and arms like iron. They dragged her forward, through an open door.

Ari had fought silently until then. The door slammed. The iron-armed man jerked a hood over her head, and she was in total darkness.

CHASE! Ari shouted, with all the force of her mind.

Milady! I am here! She heard his furious kicks at the door.

"Bar it!" a rough voice shouted. "Bar it quick,

or he'll be through it in no time. And get her hands tied behind her. Fast!"

Ari's hands were jerked behind her back and bound with thick rope. Then she heard the grating of a sliding door. Someone pushed her, hard.

And she fell forward into more darkness, sliding helplessly down a chute.

9

Ari slid a long way. She almost panicked at first. She hated having her hands tied. For a moment, she slid without thinking. Then she thrust her booted foot to the left, trying to find a wall.

Nothing. She pulled her leg back. The chute was some kind of slick metal, and she struggled to stay upright, afraid of falling over the side into — what? She twisted around, feeling safer lying on her stomach. She could feel Odie, a soft lump tucked into the hollow of her neck, and she held her head high to avoid squashing the little cat. Gradually, the chute leveled off, and finally she came to a halt.

Ari took a moment to catch her breath. Then she whispered, "Odie?"

A faint mew was her only response.

"Are you all right?"

The cat wriggled free of Ari's cloak, or at

least, Ari no longer felt her under her chin. "You got a *bag* over your head!" Odie said indignantly.

"Look around," Ari said in the softest voice she could manage. "Can you see where we are?" She took a breath. Fish. A strong smell of fish. And brine. They must be near the ocean. Odie pattered lightly over Ari's back and down her legs. For a moment, Ari couldn't feel her at all. She felt the panic coming on again. *Chase!* she shouted with her mind. *Can you hear me?*

No answer. She had fallen a long, long way indeed.

Odie's soft weight ran up her back. The cat crouched down and whispered through the hood over Ari's head. "We're in a great big room with a lot of ice and a lot of dead fish!"

So they must be in one of the warehouses down by the docks. "Is anyone else around?"

"Not yet. But there's a big, locked door at the end, and I can hear someone coming." Odie paused to listen. "There are two humans and one bird."

"Then you must hide, Odie, before they come in!"

"I'm not leaving you!"

"Just until they leave again. You're going to have to help me get untied, and I don't want you to get captured."

In the distance, a door swung open.

"I'll fight 'em!" Odie said.

"Hide!" Ari hissed. "I command it!"

69

•

She felt the cat melt away in the darkness.

"Har! We got her!" Ari recognized the voice of the man who'd demanded the door be barred. He grabbed her and set her on her feet. Ari stumbled, but stood tall. "This'll teach you to run away from your master!" The man laughed, and his voice faded a little.

He must have turned away, thought Ari. She heard the flap of wings and smelled spoiled meat. She wrinkled her nose in disgust. The man said, with an oily kind of relish that made Ari's skin prickle, "Well, we got her for you, crow! Rudy and me. Can you believe it, Rudy? A servant girl stealing that good-lookin' unicorn from her master. Now . . ." He laughed again, a bit uncertainly. "You, crow. You said that the lord was offering a reward for her capture. But I don't see no bag of gold in your beak, do you, Rudy?"

A crow? Ari thought. She remembered the black bird that had seen the Scepter lose its magic. *Dark work. There was dark work here.*

"Uh-uh," Rudy said. "I don't see no gold, Bart." He snorted with laughter.

"See, crow?" Bart again. "Rudy don't see no gold neither. And we want the reward for the capture of this thief."

"Is that what they told you?" Ari said. She was very thankful that her voice was clear and strong. "That I was a thief? A servant girl who had stolen from her master? Nonsense. Take this hood from my

70

head and see what you have done. It's you who are the thief, Rudy. And you, too, Bart."

"She knows who we are!" Rudy said, dismay running through his cloggy voice.

"She don't know nothing. She knows your name, is all. On account of I said it. Right, miss?" Bart's voice was uncertain.

"I know who I am," Ari said. "And I am no servant girl! I know who you are, too. Kidnappers! Remove this hood instantly!"

"She sounds bossy enough to be a lord herself," Rudy said timidly. "I dunno, Bart. Maybe we let this here crow talk us into something we should'na done."

"Maybe you did," Ari said icily. She felt a tentative hand on the hood. And then the crow's voice came, sharp and terrible:

"TOUCH THAT HOOD AND YOU'LL REGRET IT!"

The hand jerked away.

"Uh-oh." Rudy again. "I don't want to regret nothin'."

"Then remove yourselves," the crow said. "Both of you."

"The gold?" Bart said.

"Get out of here," the voice of the crow snarled.

Thump, slide, push: the sound of running feet.

"As you leave," the crow said evilly, "bar the door from the outside." Ari heard the sound of the door being closed and the slam of the bolt being thrown.

There was a moment of silence, when all she could hear was her own heartbeat.

"Got you *now*. Got you *now*!" The bird's cackle was filled with glee. Ari tested the rope tying her hands. It was tight. Too tight.

"And now that you've got me, what do you intend to do?" Ari said with contempt. "Take this hood off my head so that we can meet face-to-face, you coward!"

"Coward? I'll show you coward!" There was a rush of wings over her head, and the crow snatched the hood away. Ari blinked; the light was dim, and it took a moment for her eyes to adjust. She had been right. She was in a warehouse. The ceiling was low, the floor slippery with fish scales and water from melting ice. Small windows tucked under the ceiling let in the smell of the sea. The crow sat perched on a low beam above her, the hood discarded to one side.

"Who are you?" Ari demanded.

"Do you not know me, Princess?" The crow hopped sideways, its eyes a dull red. "Do you not remember me? I remember you! The last I saw of you, you were riding that monstrous beast they call the Sunchaser into the ranks of my glorious brothers. You attacked us! You wounded us! And now they are lost, all lost!"

"The Shadow unicorns," Ari said slowly. She

gazed intently at the crow. There was a familiar look to those blood-red eyes. She had seen it twice before. Just recently, when she and Chase had ridden straight into the ranks of the Shadow unicorns as they attacked the Palace. And once before, in the race for the trial by fire.

"Moloch!" she said, astonished. "You bore the Shadow Rider! He was an ally of the Shifter." She thought rapidly. No one had seen the Shadow Rider since that long-ago day in Deridia. He had not been at the battle. Could the Shadow Rider somehow have gained the Shifter's evil magic?

That didn't make sense. All magic was personal to the being who carried it. The Shifter was gone; she had seen him destroyed. So if Moloch was somehow an emissary of the Shadow Rider, there must be a new evil in Balinor.

Her heart sank.

"Yes," the crow said. "I am Moloch."

"And your new master," Ari said, keeping her voice firm so the crow wouldn't know she was guessing. "Where is he?"

The crow blinked rapidly. "He is coming!" he said slyly. "Oh, yes, he is coming! And while I wait for him, so will you! I will keep you locked here until he arrives. And there will be a new day in Balinor!"

"And when does this new master get here?" Ari asked casually.

"Oh, soon. Soon." The crow gazed upward, as if searching the sky. "And there is plenty for you to eat here while you wait. Fish. Water." His feathers shook with laughter. "Not so high and mighty now, are you, Princess!" Moloch preened his feathers with a triumphant air, then hopped along the wooden beam overhead to an open window. He fluttered his wings. "Good-bye, *milady*!"

Ari ignored the sarcasm. She noted that the opening was too small for her to wriggle through. And Rudy and Bart had locked the only door from the outside. She turned in a casual way and cast a quick glance up the chute. Maybe, just maybe. "Wait!" she snapped at the crow just before he took flight. "Aren't you going to untie me?" She kept her manner offhand. "I mean, how am I supposed to eat the fish? And you wouldn't want me to starve, would you, Moloch? You want me nice and healthy for your master, right?"

Moloch cocked his head to one side, then the other. "Oh, I don't think so," he sneered. "No, I don't think so. As a matter of fact . . ." He flew up suddenly, and, wings beating furiously, he blew out first one torch, then the other.

The warehouse plunged into total darkness. A stab of fear went through Ari. She bit her lip and took a long, slow breath.

"You can find the fish in the dark!" Moloch's voice crawled through the utter blackness. With a flutter of wings he was gone. A final caw trailed back. "Kraken is coming."

"Moloch!" Ari called into the dark.

No answer.

Ari waited a few minutes until she was sure Moloch was gone. Kraken. This new evil's name was Kraken. Then she called out in a low voice, "Odie?"

The cat patted Ari's knee. She seemed to have materialized out of nowhere. "You should have let me pounce on him," she growled. "I wanted to bite him on the neck."

"That might have worked if he were a real crow," Ari soothed. "But he's not. He has magic with him, Odie. I can sense it. He would have hurt you. Now, do you think you can help me untie my hands?" She sat down on the floor, ignoring the damp and the fish scales. She felt Odie walk delicately behind her back. Her whiskers tickled Ari's hands.

"I'm gonna grab the rope and tug it," Odie said, and so she did. She tugged and tugged, but the rope was thick, and the knot didn't budge.

"Well, this isn't going to work," Ari said after many fruitless minutes. The rope was too tight; her fingers were numb. And she was very, very cold. "Odie, I want you to open the pouch at my belt and pull out the things inside, one by one. I'm looking for a small flask. About as big around as my thumb."

Odie was more successful at opening the pouch. "Is this it?" Odie said thickly, carrying the object in her mouth. She pattered around Ari's back and dropped Atalanta's Star Bottle into her hand.

Ari curled her numb fingers around it. Atalanta had given the Star Bottle to her long ago for a situation just like this, "when all is dark about you," the Dreamspeaker had said. And it certainly was dark. Just holding something that the Dreamspeaker had given her comforted Ari.

She went into her mind, into the place where she held her personal magic. She thought of the Dreamspeaker, seemed almost to smell the perfume of roses the Celestial unicorn always carried with her.

A lovely violet light suffused the warehouse. Even the rotting fish scales sparkled.

Ari exhaled slowly, not even realizing she'd been holding her breath. "Thank goodness, Odie. At least now I can see!"

She didn't say what she was thinking. She could see. But she was still imprisoned. Still hidden away from her friends, her loved ones, with no hope of getting free.

Chase! She sent the mind-message with all the love and terror that was in her heart. *Chase!*

10

C*HASE!*

Ari's desperate cry stopped the great bronze unicorn in his tracks. He reared and plunged in the street and shouted, "Arianna!" Whinnying with joy and relief, he sent a message to his beloved Princess with all the force at his command. *MILADY! YOU ARE ALIVE!*

"What? What is it, Your Majesty?" Finn drew Beecher to a halt. "Is it the Princess? Where is she? Where is she!?"

After Ari had disappeared into the dark doorway in the alley, they had made a frantic search in the pouring rain. Chase — with Lincoln at his heels every step of the way — had kicked in the door to the hovel where Ari had been taken, but the dingy room was empty.

The five of them were wild with confusion.

What had happened to her? Where had she been taken?

It was Beecher who thought they'd been mistaken in the dark, that perhaps Ari had been dragged off into one of the many houses in this gloomy area of Sixton. Beecher and Finn persuaded the raging Sunchaser to investigate all the dilapidated places in the alley and the surrounding areas. They worked their way to the docks, where they'd met Captain Tredwell of the *Dawnwalker*, their friend in many a past adventure. He, too, had joined the search, riding pillion with Finn on Beecher. But there had been no sign of the Princess or the little cat Odie.

No sign until now, when Chase reared and cried Arianna's name.

Lori clutched Tierza's mane. "Is it Ari? Is she okay?"

Lincoln, his eyes set in a worried frown, whined under his breath.

After his first astonished relief, Chase grew grimly silent. He set off at a rapid trot toward the warehouses on the bay where the commercial fishermen docked. The others ran to keep pace behind him.

"Do you know precisely where to find the Princess, Your Majesty?" Captain Tredwell asked over Finn's shoulder as Beecher raced down the cobbled streets. "Do we need help to rescue her? I can command a half-dozen strong sailors to help in two seconds flat."

"I don't know," Chase shouted in return. "I tell

you, I don't know! If she is too far from me, I cannot hear her thoughts. So she must be near. But where? *Where?*"

CHASE!

Ari's thought hit him hard again. He skidded to a halt, sparks flying from the impact of his iron hooves on the cobblestones.

The searchers were on a small rise overlooking the warehouse. A brisk wind blew in from the sea, and the rain was a steady downpour. They could barely tell where one warehouse left off and the next one began, and there were dozens of the rotted buildings lined up and down the slope to the sea.

"Is Ari okay?" Lori ventured timidly. "She's not hurt or anything?"

"It will take forever to find her in that mess of buildings!" Finn said. His lips tightened with determination. "But we have to try."

"You don't have to try all that long to find Her Royal Highness," a familiar voice mewed out of the darkness. "Just follow me."

Lincoln broke into hysterical barking. Odie crouched down and squeezed her eyes shut.

"Easy there, Lincoln. Don't scare the kitty!" Captain Tredwell brushed his hand across his beard with a relieved sigh. "I believe the Princess has been found."

"Odie!" Lori said. "Where did you come from?"

"I came from Her Royal Highness, of course,"

the little cat said smugly. She was drenched with rain, but her yellow eyes glowed with satisfaction. "We had a terrible time, her and me, but . . ."

"Just show me —" Chase rumbled. "SHOW ME!"

Odie leaped away lightly, then trotted purposefully down a gravel path that led to a warehouse perched at the sea's edge. The others followed in single file, past heaps of discarded packing crates, fishbones, floats, and torn sails. Odie picked her way through a huge pile of trash and stopped, her tail a happy exclamation point.

"There!" she said. She nodded toward a small window set at ground level. A lovely purple light shone deep inside. "We were in that basement. I escaped through the window," she added proudly, "and set off to find you." She stuck her head in the window and yowled, "They're here!"

Ari was sitting underneath the window with her back against the wall. She jumped to her feet, shouting for joy, and in a few short minutes Finn had unbarred the outside door, and she was reunited with her friends.

Ari got an enormous, unexpected hug from Lori. Finn, too shy to express his feelings any other way, pounded Captain Tredwell on the back. The captain pounded him back. Lincoln shoved his muzzle against Ari's knees and was so happy he didn't growl at the cat.

Chase simply stood and looked at her.

You must never abandon me again, milady, he thought to her.

Ari flung her arms around his neck and breathed in his warmth. *I'm so sorry, Chase! But I was afraid if you knew that we couldn't bring the Scepter with us, you'd want to go back to Balinor and return with an army to search for the Archivist. And there's no time! No time!*

She raised her head from the warmth of his side and peered into the sky. She couldn't see the comet, not with the heavy rain clouds. But she knew it was there, streaking its slow way across the heavens. *Kraken is coming.* She went cold, even thinking the evil name.

"Let's get out of the rain, eh?" Captain Tredwell interrupted Ari and Chase unknowingly, for no one but her close friends knew about Ari's mental link with Chase. "The *Dawnwalker*'s moored not far away, and we'll get into some dry clothes there. Cook's got soup on, I'll wager, and hot oatmeal for the unicorns. And then, Your Royal Highness." His keen gray eyes searched Ari's. "Then we'll decide what's to be done."

Captain Tredwell was as good as his word. Very soon, they were warm, dry, and well fed on the *Dawnwalker*, the unicorns in their own stalls in a special area on the foredeck, Ari and the others in the captain's cabin.

"So there is a new evil coming to Balinor."

81

Captain Tredwell took a long, slow sip of hot cider. His expression was thoughtful, after Ari explained why they had been traveling in disguise without her army. "And this Archivist has the answer?"

"That is what the magic tells us. I hope to stop this Kraken, whoever — or whatever — he is," Ari said. "I must stop him. But the secret to this and other Royal matters lies with the Archivist. And we must find him — soon."

"You say this map shows you the way?"

Ari nodded. She was so exhausted she could barely keep her eyes open. Lori was fast asleep in her chair, her head tilted back and her mouth slightly open. Ari longed to be asleep, too. But she couldn't sleep. Not yet. "We must get to Shadowview — what used to be Demonview — as soon as possible," she said with a desperate edge.

The Captain tugged at his short beard. "The rain's let up some. We'll set sail tonight, Your Royal Highness. With luck, we'll be there by morning."

Soon after the captain gave the order to set sail, Ari and the others went to bed. Finn shook Lori just enough awake so that she stumbled to the cabin she shared with Ari; she fell promptly into the bunk and went right back to sleep.

But try as she might — and as tired as she was — Ari couldn't sleep. She tossed and turned so restlessly that Odie jumped off the bunk and nestled up to Lincoln, who was curled peacefully on the floor. She snuggled into the collie's thick fur, and finally, Ari fell asleep to the sounds of Odie's purr and water lapping against the hull of the ship.

As she slept, she dreamed. Atalanta came to her, violet eyes almost black with worry. In her dream, Ari reached out to the Dreamspeaker. She touched the silken mane and called out, "Atalanta!"

"Do not use the Scepter," the gentle voice echoed. "Or Kraken will find you. Kraken . . ."

"I can't use the Scepter!" Ari tried to move closer to the lovely being, to feel her warm flank under her cheek, but she was held fast by the dream magic. "The Scepter will never work again!"

"It will," Atalanta whispered. "In the time of gravest danger. Ask Archon. Ask."

"I don't understand!" Ari cried. "The Shifter's gone. But the magic in the Scepter is gone, too! I thought that all would be well in Balinor. And this evil, this . . ." She could hardly say the name. In her dream state, it seemed even more terrifying than it did in daylight.

"There is a balance in all things," Atalanta said sadly. "One side of the Deep Magic must always equal the other. You do not have the Royal Scepter now, because Kraken's power is weak. My power is weak. When Kraken grows stronger, I will grow stronger. And the Scepter may return to you, if you do not betray it."

"Why can't we just all be happy!" Ari cried. "Why does there have to be evil along with good?!"

"Ah, Arianna. Nothing in all of Balinor, or in

83

all the worlds between, works without balance." The crystal fall of the Dreamspeaker's words faded, and the silver-violet unicorn drifted away. Ari reached out. . . .

And she jerked awake. Sunlight poured through the porthole. The ship plunged steadily up and down, the ocean waves speeding by outside. It was morning. Lori was still asleep, snoring noisily. Odie woke up quietly, as cats always seem to do, and regarded her mistress with wide eyes. As hard as this journey had been, the little cat was already looking better. Sleek black fur was growing over the scars on her paws and sides, and her ribs weren't as visible as before. "Breakfast?" she said hopefully.

"It's a little early," Ari answered. "Why don't you check with Cook to see if he has some fish? And I know there'll be milk and oatmeal before long."

Odie licked her lips and bounded off. Lincoln groaned and rolled over in his sleep. Moving quietly, Ari went to her knapsack and took the Royal Scepter out of its wrapping. She held it in her hands. The shaft was cool to her touch, and the unicorn head at the top had its eyes closed. Ari sighed. How could she rule Balinor without the help of the Deep Magic? Poor Lori would never get through the Gap and to Glacier River Farm without it. And as far as this Kraken was concerned . . . Ari blinked back tears.

She should have followed the map's instructions. She knew she shouldn't have tried to second-guess the magic. She knew the Dreamspeaker was right. Atalanta was always right. Wasn't she?

There was so much at stake. She couldn't doubt her faith in the Dreamspeaker now. She would hold on. She would just hold on. Before midday, they would be within sight of Shadowview, and from there, they'd find their way to the hiding place of the Archivist.

They arrived at the Shadowview shore of the Sixth Sea just as the sun was at its height. The grim mountain towered over all, the uppermost peaks snowcapped. Just beyond the highest point, Ari saw the tail of the comet, brighter now than it had been. It was bearing down on them fast.

The three unicorns and the collie leaped over the side of the *Dawnwalker* and swam to the beach. Captain Tredwell's crew lowered the dinghy into the water and Finn, Lori, Ari, and Odie climbed in.

"You have the map?" Finn asked.

Ari touched the pouch tied to her waist. The map was there, along with the bag of small magics from Dr. Bohnes. And her precious Star Bottle, all she had at the moment of the Dreamspeaker. At least they still worked!

She had been shaken by her dream of the night before. She couldn't stop thinking. Her life as Princess would be one long, unending battle, trying to keep the balance of magic Atalanta had told her about. A difficult balance.

Not for the first time, Ari wished she could just give it all up, run away, and become a villager in Balinor. She could weave for a living, or travel to different villages singing and dancing for silver coins. She had a good voice, except that she never had time to sing anymore.

Ari lifted her face to the sun and let her thoughts drift like the ocean tide.

Chase reached the shoreline first. He climbed out of the water, his mane streaming down his neck. He glowed like a sun come to earth. His horn was a shining ebony spear. Tierza followed him. She shook her gleaming black coat free of the seawater, then rolled happily in the warm sand. Beecher ran a little way down the beach, Lincoln at his heels. The two chased each other back and forth.

It's your job to protect them. Her father, the King, had told her that, long ago, before the evil had risen in Balinor.

"And I will," Ari vowed again as the dinghy neared shore. "I will."

Chase waited for her, his thoughts steady and warm. Ari smiled at him.

Eventually, they all assembled on the beach. They waved good-bye to the *Dawnwalker*. Captain Tredwell had work to do back in Sixton, and Ari and Finn had planned on returning to Balinor by way of the long forest route. There were villages on the way that should receive news of the Shifter's defeat.

And they should be told of the new shadows in Balinor, if Ari should fail in her current quest.

Finally, they were packed up, ready for instructions, and ready to march. Ari adjusted her knapsack to a more comfortable position on her back and sat cross-legged in the sand. She pulled out the map and studied it intently.

"Well," she said more to herself than to the others. "My best guess has always been that we go to the spot marked with the comet on the map. We know that the man in the cloak was a friend, and we know that he . . . that is, the Archivist, must be found."

Ari was surprised at the doubt in her own voice. The others had stopped their low-voiced conversation and were very quiet, watching her.

"The thing is, I'm not quite sure of the best route to this teeny comet mark. The road leading up to it is marked with all kinds of little squiggles and spots."

"Those aren't squiggles and spots!"

An old man's voice? Ari stiffened and looked around uncertainly.

"I drew them myself!"

A tiny little old man stood in front of her. He had a wispy beard, a bald head, and the brightest black eyes Ari had ever seen. He was dressed in a rusty black gown. The sleeves were too short, and his bony wrists stuck out.

"Those 'squiggles and spots,' as you call them, mean danger! Humph! In the Guild of Archivists, I was well known for my elegant work! Just goes to show you that no one appreciates the finer things these days." He stopped to draw breath.

Ari was so astonished that she couldn't speak. It was the Archivist! Right here at the foot of Shadowview!

He smiled broadly, his teeth yellow with age. "Well, Princess. It's been years and years since I've seen you. You've grown more beautiful than even your lady mother. And she was the fairest I'd ever seen. It's very good to see you again."

He bent and slapped his hands against his knees. His bright black eyes looked straight at Lincoln. "And you, Gully! I quite like that disguise! I never thought to lay eyes on you again. Here, boy. Here!"

Lincoln, a wary expression in his dark brown eyes, wagged his tail slowly.

Ari found her voice. She'd known the old man, of course, the very moment she saw him. By their amused expressions, the unicorns had, too. "Archon! Why, wherever in the world did you come from?"

11

❧

"I made myself quite a tidy little nest in the tunnels under the mountain!" Archon said. "After the day of the Great Betrayal I fled. I had to leave Gully, of course." He reached out and patted Lincoln's ears. Lincoln quietly backed away.

They all followed him across the sand. He trudged on ahead, his cheerful chatter like a stream in full flood.

Chase looked doubtfully up at the mountain. "Why here?" he rumbled. "This mountain was the gate to the very seat of the Shifter's power — the Valley of Fear."

"Now it's called Terra Incognita, Your Majesty," Archon said. "I reworked the map myself. Here! Here's the door to my home!" He pushed aside a large thorny bush, rolled two boulders aside, and a trapdoor in the sand was revealed to the travelers' amazed eyes. "And why here? Because this is where

89

everything seemed to start. I have my helpers, you know. The seagulls, the sand turtles, the little foxes that live on the sides of the mountain. They knew where to find me, and they brought me all the news."

He pulled up the trapdoor and turned to face Ari. He looked very apologetic. "I was aware when you and the Sunchaser passed by on your quests. But I couldn't come out." He shook his head. "No, I couldn't come out to help you. I am a historian, you know, a mere observer of events. And the Shifter would have made mincemeat of me in two seconds flat! Not to mention that he would have stolen all I had saved from the Royal Archives. And if he'd gotten those claws of his on the knowledge contained there . . . brrrh!"

He shuddered, then stepped aside. A long flight of steps had been dug into the sand. "Welcome! Welcome! Please! Follow me. Come along, Gully."

"His name's Lincoln," Lori said. "Not Gully."

Archon's eyes twinkled. He opened his mouth as if about to speak, then closed it. "Lincoln, hmm? We shall see. Come along. Come along."

Finn insisted on leading the way. Chase and Beecher walked behind him. Ari put Odie on her shoulder. Lincoln, Lori, and Tierza trailed behind.

The stairs were broad and shallow. It seemed to Ari that they descended into the earth a long, long way. The steps ended in a broad, white gravel path. Torches lined the walls painted with lively scenes of Balinor activities. Ari saw a beautiful drawing of the Royal court, with her mother and father on the throne. She was there, too, in her velvet chair, no more than seven years old. Her older brother Bren was beside her. "These are wonderful, Archon," she called.

"Those? Yes. Well, I had a lot of time on my hands. It took an awfully long time to defeat the Shifter, Your Royal Highness."

They passed more drawings and paintings. Some were familiar: farmers working the fields, the Great Midsummer Fair, the Samletts at the Unicorn Inn. But some were unfamiliar, the paintings of wizard laboratories in particular. "Oh, in the old days, I had all sorts of friends," Archon said merrily. "And not all of them in Balinor, mind you. There are many doors in the Gap, which lead to many lands. Before the Shifter took over, I used to visit quite often. Gully knows, don't you, Gully?"

Lincoln pressed his head into Ari's hand. She fondled his ears, smoothing the furry tips with a gentle hand. She could feel the big dog tremble. "It's all right, Linc."

"It's not." His soft brown eyes looked up at her worriedly. "I will never leave you, Ari! I vowed never to leave you!"

"Nobody said anything about leaving," Ari said, puzzled. What was going on with her dog? But before she could ask, they came to the end of the tunnel.

A large wooden door filled the entire end of

the tunnel. Archon took a huge iron key from a pocket in his gown, unlocked it, and flung it open. "And here we are!" Archon said proudly. "My little nest. Come in. Come in. Have a seat."

"Ah, where?" Lori asked sarcastically.

Ari — although she deplored Lori's blunt rudeness — couldn't help but wonder where, indeed. Archon's little nest was a frantic mess of papers, bits of dried flowers, seashells, balled-up paper . . . and books. Thousands and thousands of books. Books towered in shaky piles to the ceiling. They spilled in erratic stacks all over the dirt floor. And on top of the books, in every possible corner, were piles of paper, neatly bound with ribbon.

A fire burned brightly in a corner fireplace. A pot hung over the flames. Whatever was in it had boiled over — Ari guessed it was stew — and crusted the sides. A huge clock ticked slowly on the mantel. It was a few moments before Ari realized that the pendulum swung far more slowly than a normal clock's. She examined the face; the hands of the clock were actually fingers made of bronze. And instead of numbers to count the hours, twelve figures danced in a circle.

"That is curious," she observed.

Archon glanced at the clock. "My goodness! I had no idea! Well, there's a bit of time left. We must hurry, though, Princess." The look of concern quickly vanished, however, and he gestured expansively. "Come in! Come in!"

92

Tierza looked carefully around the entire room. She pawed delicately at a tangle of birds' nests near the door. "You know," Tierza said in a brightly sociable way, "I think Beecher and I want another look at those wall paintings, Archon. You don't mind if we wander around a bit, do you?"

"I'll go with you," Lori said hastily. "You go ahead and get your business done. You can tell us all about it later." Lori and the two Royal unicorns went out the door. Ari motioned that Finn should also leave; he reluctantly joined Lori in the passageway. It swung closed behind them, but not before Lori's voice floated back: "How can he *live* in that mess?"

Archon wrung his hands. He looked around his "cozy little nest" unhappily, as if seeing it with fresh eyes. "Oh, Your Royal Highness. I didn't stop to think." He glanced swiftly at the clock. "What with time running out and all. . . . Why, when I saw that you were coming, I should have cleaned up."

"I think your room is very cozy," Ari said kindly. "Now, Archon. Chase and I are here for a reason. We have serious matters to attend to in Balinor."

The Archivist blinked rapidly at her. "Of course! The comet! Coming closer and closer all the while I dither on. And I have what you need to stop it."

"We have to stop the comet?" Ari said. "Is that possible?"

"Well, now let me see. No, no, you'll not stop the comet. You'll stop the comet from pouring its magic into Kraken. If you don't — well . . ." Archon paused and scratched his head. "Then we'll have a new evil in Balinor. A lot worse than the other one, if you ask me. This is what you've come to do, milady," he said simply. "And you must do it."

"I'll try," Ari said steadily. "Chase and I must always try. But can you help us?"

"That's why you've come to find me, isn't it? Now, it's *somewhere* around here. I was examining it just the other day. . . ." He began to scrabble through the mess on the floor. Odie hopped down from Ari's shoulder and poked around with him.

Ari watched Archon and thought at Chase. *How is the Archivist going to help us defeat Kraken? How are we going to get the magic flowing through the Royal Scepter again? And how are we going to get Lori home?*

The great unicorn's eyes crinkled in concern and amusement.

"Here it is!" Archon dug through a loose mound of papers. A parchment titled "Correspondence Between Queen Asteride and Prince Dunmorton" flew into the soup kettle. Lincoln dashed forward and snatched it out with his jaws. Finding nowhere else to put it, he dropped it on the floor.

Archon emerged from the litter with an object the size of a breadfruit clutched in both hands and shouted, "The Watcher's Crystal Ball!"

Reverently, he set it on the floor. Ari walked over and looked down. The crystal ball was made of

94

a solid glasslike substance the color of fresh milk. Odie sniffed at it curiously.

"Is it . . . is it like the Watching Pool in the Celestial Valley?" Ari asked. "Will I be able to see places and people from far away?"

Archon danced a little jig around the room. "That's it, exactly."

Ari picked it up. It felt like a giant marble. "I don't recall this," she said.

"Well, you wouldn't. The Palace has never had one before. But I picked it up on one of my little side trips when I was visiting some friends. This was before the day of the Great Betrayal, you understand. Since then, without Gully . . . well, I haven't been able to go, of course. And it's too bad. It's affected my collection. An Archivist collects all sorts of things, you know. I mean, I'm responsible for the Royal family's documents, deeds, and correspondence, but I archive lots of other things as well. I have a very nice book of spells somewhere around here."

The clock on the mantel struck once: a hollow, almost ghostly chime. Archon jumped as if he'd been stung by a bee. "It's late!" he exclaimed. "Come! There's no time to lose!" He snatched up the Watcher's Crystal Ball, grabbed a scruffy hat off a chair loaded with garments of various kinds, and headed straight for the fireplace. "Your Majesty! Your Royal Highness! Gully! Come on!"

Archon rapped the base of the clock with his knuckle, and the entire fireplace swung slowly forward. A wooden door with a carved peak was re-vealed.

Ari had seen doors like that before. She had been through the Gap several times; doors like this lined the way. They were doors to other lands, and she had vowed once to find time to explore them all. But now? And without the aid of the Scepter?

"Now, Gully," the Archivist said. "Open it, please."

Lincoln walked forward. His mahogany-and-cream coat glowed in the light of the fire. He turned and gave Ari the saddest, most miserable glance she had ever seen.

"What is it, Linc? What's wrong?"

He stood in front of the door, threw back his head, and sang. She had never heard that sound from him before; it was high and strong, like a wolf's howl in the far reaches of winter. It was beautiful, in the way that very strong things can be beautiful: ma-jestic, mournful, and magnificent all at once.

The door swung open. A fair green garden beckoned to them. Ari glimpsed a fountain, trickling clear water, and the sweep of a jeweled humming-bird's wings.

Odie squeaked in dismay and burrowed safely under a pile of letters.

"This is Bloom." Archon rubbed his hands in a kind of sad satisfaction. "Thank you, Gully. This is exactly where we need to be. Bloom is a land of re-newal, Your Royal Highness. In Bloom, all magic works. As you know, Gully, when we go in you will start from the beginning. So your spell isn't going to work anymore."

Lincoln hung his head and closed his eyes.

"I don't understand." Ari held the Watcher's Crystal Ball tightly. For some reason, she was very nervous. "What spell? How did you open this door, Linc? It's a door to the Gap! The only way to open doors into other lands to the Gap is with the help of the Deep Magic. How did you do it?"

Lincoln sat down. His creamy ruff stirred with a faint breeze from the land beyond the door. "I hoped this day would never come," he said sadly. "I was the one who brought you through the Gap the first time, milady. I am the key to all the lands that lead to the Gap.

"I am the Link."

12

They stepped into a garden more glorious than Ari had ever seen before.

Fragrant lilies nodded next to the fountain. Hyacinth flourished under banks of spicy-scented dianthus. Jasmine and ginger nestled in the stone paths.

"Bloom," Archon said in a matter-of-fact way. "Every flower known to the worlds grows here. Now, Your Royal Highness, flowers are not the only things that flourish in this land. In this place, time lags. This land is at least three days behind Balinor, which is why I brought you here, of course, because in this land, the Scepter has not lost its power to channel your personal magic." Worry creased his face. "At least, it *should* work. But you never know with the Old Mare."

But Ari was listening with only half an ear. She stood next to Chase and stared at her dog.

Or what had been her dog.

A squat, toadlike creature crouched where her beautiful collie had been. Ari had never seen its like before. But the dark brown eyes were familiar, and so was the wistful look. She knelt in front of the creature. "Lincoln?" she said softly. A transforming spell! Her collie had been under a transforming spell! "Who *are* you, Linc?"

"Gully," the creature said. Only it was a frog-like croak, not Lincoln's beloved voice. "My name is Gully!"

The toad squatted down. Two tears rolled down his cheeks. "I wanted to be with the Princess," he said to the Archivist. "It's a lonely business, being the Link to all the worlds. You don't see all that many people. And when the Dreamspeaker herself came to me and asked for help . . . and you were so lost and hurt, milady."

He hopped forward. "At any rate, the balance of magic was way off when the Dreamspeaker came to me for help after the day of the Great Betrayal. They had to hide you and the Sunchaser from the Shifter. And the best place was Glacier River Farm. No one ever goes there from here. It's a hard place. No magic at all. And I said, of course, I would take Her Royal Highness through the Gap to Glacier River Farm. But when I got there — I didn't want to go back. So I hid from the Dreamspeaker and everyone else.

"I had just one spell with me. Just one. A

transforming spell. I'd picked it up when I escorted you to Mirrin, Archon."

"Oh, yes? Hmm. You shouldn't have taken the spell, my boy. Might not have worked outside of Mirrin. Or it could have turned you into something even ug — I mean . . . never mind. What's done is done."

"When you look like I do," Gully said wryly, "you take chances. When Ari and the Sunchaser were on the other side at the farm — well, I just decided not to go back. I used the spell. And ever since then, no one but you knew who I really was, Archon." He looked up at Ari, and all of his love and loyalty were in that look. "I couldn't leave the Princess, you see. She was so hurt — so broken. She needed me to defend her!"

Then Gully turned to Chase. "You didn't even remember who you were! So I stayed. And yes, that meant that it was almost impossible to get through the Gap without a great deal of Deep Magic, but the Dreamspeaker thought that the Shifter had kidnapped the Link, and the Shifter thought the Dreamspeaker had hidden me, and nobody really thought about fixing it because so much else was going on. I don't think," he added, "that it affected matters too much. Perhaps it did. Anyhow. If I must be punished, I am ready."

Archon tugged at his beard. Then he stared at the sky. Even here, the comet loomed above them. "No time for punishment. No time for anything. It's coming," he muttered. "Even here, it's coming. There's no time for this, Gully. Not now. Quick, Your Royal Highness. The ball! The Deep Magic should work here! Look into the Watcher's Ball!"

Ari took a deep breath. She held the crystal ball in front of her and went into her personal magic. She gazed into it, Chase beside her. The ball began to buzz like a hive of bees, and she nearly dropped it in alarm. An image spun around and around in the milky depths. It whirled so fast that she couldn't make it out. And then . . .

Moloch's bloodred eyes seemed to stare straight into hers! She steadied herself against Chase and held on. The horrible crow didn't see her; he was looking up to the comet coming ever closer.

"Do you see?" Archon asked anxiously. "Do you see where the comet will strike? No, no. It does no good to hold the ball out to me, Princess. It will not work for anyone but a member of the Royal family."

"It looks like the Valley of Fear," Ari said slowly. "Or what used to be the Valley of Fear."

"Terra Incognita," Chase said. "The crow — Moloch — is in the Pit. And see there, milady. In the sand."

Ari shuddered. The crow hopped around and around at the very bottom of the Pit. And something — something was trying to claw its way up out of the sand.

Overhead, the comet flamed nearer. The Pit

glowed with a sickly yellow-green light as the head of the comet passed close overhead. In the lurid light, Moloch's feathers glistened with an oily sheen.

"So that's where it is? Where Kraken will emerge? The Pit?" Archon's kindly face grew stern. The image in the ball died away.

Ari put the ball away in the pouch at her waist and nodded in answer to Archon's question. "Yes," she said simply. "And we must go there?"

"We must go there now!" Archon said. "As fast as possible. I have read of this in the histories of the Royal family, milady. Kraken will emerge in his full power if you do not divert the course of the comet with the Deep Magic!"

"We have no time!" Ari said. "It is a long way up Shadowview and down the other side! And the Scepter . . ." She exchanged a worried look with Chase. Would the Scepter come alive? The Dream-speaker had promised. But who knew what terrible things this new evil could accomplish!

It doesn't matter, Chase thought at her. *Whatever happens, we must be there.*

Ari nodded. "We have to try. Even if we are too late, we have to try."

"You won't be too late," Gully said. "There is a way. A shortcut through the Gap itself. I will show you."

Ari left the fragrance of Bloom with scarcely a thought to its beauty. Gully hopped rapidly through flowers and shrubs whose loveliness would have been overwhelming if she had not been so determined to complete the task ahead. They went quickly through a door to leave Bloom, which took them to a land of snow, blue ice, and granite mountains. From there, they passed through an alien forest so still Ari could hear the grass thrusting up through the mossy floor, and then . . .

They arrived at a place that Ari and Chase had been before. A place Ari had hoped never to see again.

The Pit in the Valley of Fear.

They stepped through a door nearly at the bottom of the Pit. The comet's light cast an eerie yellow-green shadow, twisting the rocks and thornbushes into weirdly malignant shapes. Slightly below them, Moloch hopped from one claw to the other, his eyes staring fiercely at a roiling whirlpool of sand.

Archon yelped and hid behind a rock. Ari drew the Royal Scepter from her knapsack. It was inert; no pulse of magic came to her.

"Please," Gully said. "Please take me with you!" His eyes, so like her collie's eyes, gazed up at her from his warty face.

"It will be dangerous," Ari murmured.

"I don't care!"

Wordlessly, Ari picked up the small toad and settled him in the recesses of her cloak. He was Lincoln, no matter what his form. And it was right that the three of them be together.

Chase bent his great head and rested his

muzzle on her hair. The bronze of his coat shone as bright as fire in the ugly light. Then he knelt. Ari mounted, and Chase picked his way carefully down the slope. Moloch, his gaze intent upon the Pit where Kraken would emerge, did not yet see them.

With a feeling of hopelessness, Ari held the Scepter aloft. Still no rosy light. No reassuring warmth to flood her hands and direct her magic.

The wind picked up as the comet drew near. The very rocks began to throb with the advent of its power. Moloch hopped eagerly from claw to claw. But something alerted him. He craned his neck and saw Ari and Chase. With a scream of rage, he beat his wings and flew into the air.

And with the last of his magic, he transformed himself into his true form: Moloch, the Shadow unicorn.

His eyes rolled red in his gaunt and ghastly face, and he pawed the ground in battle lust. His horn was thick, gnarled, sharpened to a deadly point at the end. The wild wind whipped his mane and forelock around his face. He charged up the slope at them.

With a rush of mighty winds, the comet's head appeared over the Pit. And with a great cry, Moloch leaped forward.

Chase gathered his hindquarters and sprang to meet the Shadow unicorn. Their horns clashed and they fought like swordsmen, parrying, lunging, spearing.

Through it all, Ari stayed on Chase. She clung to the saddle, holding the Scepter steady, her eyes intent upon the place where Kraken would appear.

The comet's terrible heat burst upon the Pit. A long-nailed hand crawled from the sand. Yellow-green light leaped from the upthrust fingers —

And suddenly, the Scepter sprang to life!

Ari felt the power run down her arm and through her. She concentrated all of her will into the shining wand and cried out, "BACK! I SEND YOU BACK!"

The hand trembled. The rosy light of the Scepter surrounded the green-yellow of evil. But the hand grasped the edge of the rocky sand and clawed its way to the surface. The hand twisted, spread, and the light of the comet filled the palm.

"He's getting the magic from the comet!" Ari yelled to Chase. She clutched his mane and slid to the ground. "I must go, Chase! I have to destroy the hand!"

But the mighty unicorn fought on, unable to leave the battle. Moloch was a great warrior. His horn slashed great wounds on the Sunchaser's chest.

"He will drag you down with him!" Gully said. Without warning, Gully suddenly jumped from her cloak and hopped down the slope of the Pit before Ari could stop him.

The small toad didn't hesitate. He jumped into Kraken's hand. The fingers closed involuntarily. Ari lost no time. She directed the full power of the Scepter up, up to the comet.

The rosy light engulfed the green! With a rush and an incredible roar of sound, the comet passed by.

The light was gone.

Kraken's hand withered and then disappeared.

But there was no sign of Gully.

There was no time to look for him. Moloch and Chase fought on. Chase finally brought the Shadow unicorn to his knees and, with a final, terrifying thrust of his horn, drove him onto his back.

"Do you yield?" Chase asked sternly.

"I yield." The mad red light was gone from Moloch's eyes. In its place was defeat.

Chase backed up. He took great breaths of air. Sweat streamed down his neck. "Milady? What is your wish?" He held his horn straight at Moloch's evil heart.

The Scepter spread its forgiving glow around them all. "Let him go," Ari said softly. "There's been enough war. Let him go."

Moloch turned and ran.

Terra Incognita was still. The comet was a pale green rush on the horizon, headed for other places. Ari sat on the ground and took several deep breaths. Then she took the salve from her pouch and treated the wounds on Chase's flanks and sides.

"You were lucky," she said soberly. "These wounds are superficial."

Archon peeked timidly from behind his boulder.

"You can come out now." Ari smiled at him. "It's safe."

"I have never seen the like, Your Royal Highness! What a battle! It was glorious!"

Ari put the salve away. Her heart was heavy, despite the victory. "We must look for Lincoln — I mean Gully."

Chase trotted forward and nosed at the place where Kraken's hand had been. She heard a faint croak. "Here, milady."

Ari went to Chase's side. Gully stared up at her. She bent and picked him up, cradling him softly in her hands. "Oh, Lincoln, Lincoln. Are you hurt?"

"Just a little squashed!" he croaked bravely. "I jumped, just before Kraken closed his fist." The little toad trembled. "He was cold! So cold!"

Archon fussed with his beard. "If you're feeling up to it, my boy, you should get us back to my little nest."

Gully struggled to stand in Ari's hand.

"Give him a moment," Ari said.

"No. No. Let's get out of this place." He took a small hop. "The way out is over there. You remember, milady. Lori fell through the Gap here once before."

The way back was different. Ari wasn't sure why. But she scarcely noticed the changing landscapes and only really paid attention when they were once again in Archon's chambers. It was if they had never left.

Lori, Finn, and the Royal unicorns were still

wandering around in the passage outside the Archivist's home. Odie was curled asleep on a pile of discarded boots. And the place was still a mess. Odie bounced over to Ari when they came through the fireplace, mewing loudly.

Archon peered hopefully into the pot of stew still bubbling over the fire. "I would like to offer you some lunch, Your Royal Highness. But someone seems to have eaten most of the stew!" He glared at Odie.

"It wasn't me!" she said indignantly. She burped. Ari stifled a laugh.

"It must have boiled away, I think," Ari said. She still held Lincoln, or Gully, as she supposed she must call him now.

"You look so sad!" Archon said. "I'm sorry about the stew."

"It doesn't matter." Ari caressed Gully with the tip of her finger. A faint chime of bells caught her attention and she looked around, puzzled. "Is that the clock, Archon?"

"The clock? No, no. It's the Watcher's Crystal Ball, milady!" His mild face beamed with excitement. "I do believe . . . yes, I do believe —"

Ari drew the ball out. The colors in it were swirling violet and shimmering crystal. She stared into the depths and the sound of chiming bells grew clearer. After a moment, the lovely form of the Dreamspeaker appeared.

"Atalanta!" Ari cried. She set the ball on the mantel, where they all could see the Dreamspeaker.

"You have done well, my child." The deep purple eyes gazed at Ari's face. "You all have done well. You, the Sunchaser and Princess Arianna, have defeated one of the greatest enemies to ever threaten Balinor!"

Atalanta stood at the edge of the Watching Pool in the Celestial Valley. The Rainbow herd stood behind her, horns held high, all their colors glowing. "Hail, Princess Arianna!" they cried. "Hail, Sunchaser!"

The cheering died away. "But we still need to rescue my parents," Arianna said. "We will," Atalanta replied. "One day soon we will." A slight smile crossed Atalanta's face. "Now," she said with pretend sternness. "Gully! Set him here, next to me, Arianna."

Ari carefully placed the little toad on the mantel next to the crystal ball. He quivered and crouched down, shutting his eyes tight. "You, sir, have caused us great concern. We have no other Link to the Gap!"

"I am sorry, Dreamspeaker!"

"I wish you'd said something," Atalanta returned. "I don't know what I can do to find another Link. It is not the business of the Celestial Valley to govern the Gap. But I *can* do this. Hop down, Gully, to the floor."

The little toad looked down with a dubious air. It was a long way down for someone his size.

"Do as I say, Gully." The Dreamspeaker's tone brooked no argument. Ari bit back a cry of alarm.

Gully took a breath, squeezed his eyes shut, and leaped.

He jumped *slowly.* Ari watched, puzzled, as Gully fell toward the floor. It was as if he jumped through molasses or mud. And as he fell, he grew larger and larger. His legs grew long. His nose lengthened to a furry point. His ears grew up into a tulip shape. And his warty hide changed into a glorious mahogany and cream.

"Lincoln!" Ari cried. She ran forward and cradled her beautiful collie in her arms. Lincoln stared down at his little white forepaws. He wagged his tail faster and faster. He barked, and barked again, the noise filling the room.

Chase rumbled happily. Archon clapped his hands. Odie sulked and ran under a battered chair.

Ari was smiling so hard her cheeks hurt. She looked up at the mantel and said, "Oh, thank you, Atalanta! Thank you!"

But the Watcher's Crystal Ball was solid white. The Dreamspeaker was gone.

"What's all the barking?" Lori marched in, Finn and the Royal unicorns at her heels. "Are we ready to go yet? I've looked at all those pictures till my eyes bugged out!"

"Yes, Lori." Ari buried her hands in Lincoln's creamy ruff and laughed for happiness. "We are going home to Balinor!"

"So I don't have to go back to Glacier River Farm?" Lori's face brightened. "I can still be your lady-in-waiting?"

"We'll wait a while yet," Ari said. "We need to find a new Link to the Gap. And until we get one, you can stay."

"Good!" Lori said. "I've been meaning to talk to you about a couple of new outfits, Ari, old pal, old friend."

Ari hugged her collie. She looked deep into Chase's eyes. There would still be tough times ahead in Balinor. She saw that now. There would never be a time when she could completely relax. No Princess ever could.

But she had her friends around her.

And no Princess could ask for more than that!

About the Author

Mary Stanton loves adventure. She has lived in Japan, Hawaii, and all over the United States. She has held many different jobs, including singing in a nightclub, working for an advertising agency, and writing for a TV cartoon series. Mary lives on a farm in upstate New York with some of the horses who inspire her to write adventure stories like the UNICORNS OF BALINOR.

Rockett's World ™

GET READY!
GET SET!
READ ROCKETT!

$3.99 US each

- ❑ BDT 0-439-04405-7 **#1: Who Can You Trust?**
- ❑ BDT 0-439-06312-4 **#2: What Kind of Friend Are You?**
- ❑ BDT 0-439-08209-9 **#3: Are We There Yet?**
- ❑ BDT 0-439-08210-2 **#4: Can You Keep a Secret?**
- ❑ BDT 0-439-08694-9 **#5: Where Do You Belong?**
- ❑ BDT 0-439-08695-7 **#6: Who's Running This Show?**

Available wherever you buy books, or use this order form.

Scholastic Inc., P.O. Box 7502, Jefferson City, MO 65102

Please send me the books I have checked above. I am enclosing $_____ (please add $2.00 to cover shipping and handling). Send check or money order–no cash or C.O.D.s please.

Name_____Birth date_____

Address_____

City_____State/Zip_____

Please allow four to six weeks for delivery. Offer good in U.S.A. only. Sorry, mail orders are not available to residents of Canada. Prices subject to change.